THE RELUCTANT INCUMBENT

JACK R. STANLEY

WRIGHTBRIDGE PRESS

The Reluctant Incumbent
by
Jack R. Stanley

Text copyright © 2015 by Jack R. Stanley
All rights reserved.
This book may not be copied or reproduced, in whole or in part, by any means, electronic, mechanical or otherwise, without written permission from the publisher except by a reviewer who may quote brief passages in his/her review.

This is a work of fiction. Any resemblance to any persons, events or localities is purely coincidental and beyond the intent of the author and publisher.

Credits:
Cover illustration: iStock belterz
Edited by Mary Lee Stanley

jacks@wrightbridgepress.com
www.http:jackrstanley.com
www.http:/thefictionwritersnotebook.com

❀ Created with Vellum

DEDICATION

To Mary Lee
The love of my life.
And
to my sister-in-law,
Rose Marie,
who, when we were visiting there,
left me the hell alone
so I could write.

FREE E-BOOKS

GET TWO FREE E-NOVELS
BY
JACK R. STANLEY

MURDER IN MULESHOE, murder in a modern small Texas town, and GUNS ALONG THE RIO, historic western action/adventure.

http://eepurl.com/dKEi_Y

CHAPTER 1

Anyone who thinks he or she wants to be President of the United States doesn't have any grasp of what the job is, what responsibilities it encompasses, nor the sheer weight that falls on whoever holds that title. Fifty-one year old Vice President Sundee Ives understood. When she had accepted President Porter Randall's invitation to have her name submitted to Congress as his V.P., she was in her second term as Governor of New Hampshire. It was her husband, history professor and former Naval intelligence officer, Oliver Ives who had convinced his lovely wife to accept the post as her duty as a citizen that had put her where she was today.

She sat in the Vice President's office in what Mark Twain had once described as "the ugliest building in America," the Eisenhower Executive Office Building, just west of the White House between Pennsylvania and New York Avenues. The structure was designed in the French Second Empire style and was commissioned by President .U.S. Grant. It had been built between 1887 and 1888. The building, originally intended to house the Departments of War, State, as well as the Department of the Navy, had also been the site of White House stables. Located on 17th Street NW, between Pennsylvania and New York Avenues, and West Executive Drive, the almost gaudy edifice had been used by President Porter Randall temporarily when he was first thrust into the most powerful position in the world following the sudden death of his predecessor, Democrat Leo V. Gibson.

Vice President Ives thought of all the horse shit that had originated or passed through the building's walls in subsequent years since the building was erected. And here she was trying to keep her head above political manure following the assassination attempt on President Randall. He lay in a coma in what was officially the largest military medical complex in the world --- what had once been Bethesda Naval Medical Center and Walter Reed Army Hospital --- now Walter Reed National Military Medical.

The late President Gibson, ever the consummate manipulator and deal maker, had failed to name a new Vice President following the sudden resignation of William Mandel who was caught in the Internet Scandal known as Net-Gate. Also swept up in the corruption were two cabinet secretaries, nine Senators and the Speaker of the House. A former Texas surgeon turned medical thriller novelist after the sudden tragic death of his wife in a plane crash, Porter Randall was a two term U.S. House Representative when he had been appointed Speaker of the House. The reason for his election to the post came when competing factions of the Republican Caucus couldn't break a deadlock on the day Congress was set to adjourn. The deal was Randall, who had no enemies on either side of the struggle for power, would be officially named to the position so that he could adjourn Congress for its scandal delayed Christmas recess. In January, when all the behind the scene deal makings and arm twisting were done, Randall was to step aside and the designated winner of the tussle would assume the office. However, President Gibson died suddenly of a cerebral hemorrhage only days after Christmas in California.

The new and temporary, but very official Speaker of the House, was awakened at his Amarillo home in the early morning hours and informed that he was now the President of the United States. Months later, Sundee Ives was in the same position, reluctantly assuming the mantel of great power and the burdens which accompanied it when President Randall had been shot delivering a speech in an airport hangar in Milwaukee two days after delivering his first State of The Nation address.

Congressional recall elections were underway in all but two states based on President Randall's address. His Executive Order symbolically ending the nonsense of political correctness had struck a resounding note with the public as did his calling for English Only for anyone dealing with the Executive Branch. The new President was well received by the American public and profoundly shocked at his attempted murder.

The bullet intended to kill fifty-two year old President Porter Randall had instead missed his heart because he had shifted his weight to his right foot an instant before impact. His director of Communication, thirty-five year old Cinnamon Higdon, had stuck an index finger down into the President's chest to stem the pulsing blood squirting from his chest. The mixed race beauty, first in her class at Stanford University School of Law, had leaped to the President's body where he fell on the risers in the airport hangar. As Secret Service agents and medical techs rushed to help, Cinnamon stopped the gushing of the President's blood. His head was in her lap on the gurney and his blood on her clothes as together they were wheeled to the belly of Air Force One.

There an on-board emergency surgical team could do everything possible even in a level one trauma center. When Cinnamon's digit was removed and the surgeon stopped the bleeding, the President's second injury was discovered. Porter had struck the back of his head on the metal corner of the risers behind him. The President was immediately placed into a medically induced coma until the cerebral damage could be assessed and treated in D.C.

The instant the President was stable the huge aircraft began to roll and was airborne in less than two minutes.

Vice President Sundee Ives was notified and assumed the powers of Acting President. It was under the same amendment, The Presidential Succession Amendment, which had propelled Porter Randall into the office only months before that now enabled Ives to take office.

This time, the Vice President invoked the provisions of Section 4 and notified the members of the cabinet, the President pro tempore of the Senate and the Speaker of the House. Then, by written declaration signed by all these principals stating that the President was unable to discharge the powers and duties of his office, and Mrs. Sundee Ives assumed the title of Acting President and all that went with it.

One day later two London to Paris under-the-English-Channel Eurostar trains were attacked by terrorists. One thousand twenty-seven passengers and crew lost their lives as the Chunnel collapsed from twin explosions, one each on different trains headed in different directions at the time of blasts.

CHAPTER 2

"Thanks for giving me the finger."

Reportedly those were the last words of President Randall before he lapsed into unconsciousness as the gurney thumped its way towards Air Force One. His Director of White House Communications was looking into his fluttering eyes, his head in her lap.

That had been two months ago.

Doctor Leonard Millhuff, a slight man even in full surgical cap, gown, and mask, was the personal physician of the previous president, Leo Gibson, who had been asked to stay at his post by the new Chief Executive. Aboard Air Force One, Dr. Millhuff had stabilized Porter, extracted Cinnamon's finger from his chest and stanched the flow of blood from his chest. The small man had opened the President's left chest, discovered that the bullet had pierced the pericardium, the double-walled sac that protects the heart against infection, as well as providing it with lubrication within the chest. The projectile had then gone on to nick the left atrium, the upper left pumping chamber of the organ.

Working frantically but with detached professionalism, the surgical team was able to suture all the openings with staples and pack the area around the wounds to absorb any leakage. The goal was to stop the loss of the vital fluid, blood, and enable the body to begin its own healing. Dr. Millhuff was reminded of the old quote often used by his professors in medical school, "God heals but the physicians get the fees."

One of the surgical nurses was the one who pointed out the gash on the back of the President's head. After a cursory exam of the injury, Dr. Millhuff called for the immediate injection of Depotherazine, a long half-life barbiturate. Usually administered intramuscularly, the drug was designed to induce a medical coma and slow the brain's function down. Millhuff's primary specialty was general abdominal surgery although his secondary field was internal medicine. He was no brain specialist, but he did know that to prevent permanent damage to brain tissue. The prescribed treatment was to reduce the energy requirements of the brain. The objective would be to protect any brain tissue which, due in whole or in part to the wound, might be on the edge of oxygen starvation. The additional dose of the drug, Mannltol, was administered. This second medication was a strong diuretic known to pull water out of the brain to temporarily decrease the intracranial pressure. It was the best Dr. Millhuff could do until they were able to get the President to Walter Reed and a brain specialist.

What had perplexed the specialist was the continued coma state in which the President remained long after the withdrawal of the drugs. Clearly there must have been some injury which was not apparent on the CT or MRI scans.

Porter's sister, Irene, met her husband, Mark Meehan, at the medical center. Mark had telephoned Porter's daughter Page and her husband, Kirk Schultz, both physicians and faculty members at Texas Tech Medical School in Lubbock. The family set up around the clock rotations in the Intensive Care Unit so that Porter was never alone. The group enlarged by one when Secret Service Agent Melissa McBride allowed Deidra McAffie, to join the family.

Agent McBride had been the one who discreetly took Deidra from Porter Randall's house to her ranch in Amarillo the night Porter was informed that the mantle of the Presidency had fallen to him. The lovely fifty year old widow of Porter's former surgical partner projected a kindness and peace which only comes from within.

Deidra was trying to convince Porter that it was time he got out of his self-imposed exile and rejoin life. She, with the help of an excellent wine and some alluring lingerie, had succeeded in getting him to bed where they both found again a part of their lives they had put on hold following the sudden death of their respective spouses.

It was Deidra whom Porter had phoned when the press raised questions about some of his military metals which, on his resume, he didn't claim nor did he display in his office. She had gone back to Porter's house and located the trunk where his Purple Heart and two Silver Stars were stored. They were professionally framed and now sat on a console behind the President's desk.

Over the days and weeks of waiting, Deidra had become the person who spent more time on watch than anyone else. She took her assigned shift but was also there almost every waking hour holding Porter's hand when it was free and boosting the spirits of the family.

There was a spark of hope when the breathing tube was removed and the President continued to breathe on his own. However, he simply failed to regain consciousness. The vigil continued.

Deidra was asleep with her face on the sheets of his bed, her hand in his, her face turned toward the foot of the bed, when Porter first awoke.

As the cobwebs began to clear, he was able to see that he was in a hospital room, Porter kept blinking and licking his lips. He freed his hand from Deidra's and was able to identify another tube running under his nose. For a full minute he just focused on breathing and trying to get his bearings. From the sheen of her chestnut hair he knew it was Deidra. Taking more effort than he thought it should require, he lifted his hand and gently stroked her soft tresses.

Instantly Deidra was awake, twisting to look at Porter and shooting to her feet as she took his face in her hands.

"Porter?" she asked peering into his eyes. "Are you awake?"

He took a breath and managed to say, "I think that's what they call it. Water?"

Deidra smothered his cheek with kisses before she picked up the plastic glass with the remains of what had once been a full glass of ice chips. She aimed the straw to his lips and he took a sip. Deidra punched the call button at the end of the cord clipped to the edge of his pillow.

"Yes?" came the voice of the call nurse.

"The President is awake!" Deidra announced.

CHAPTER 3

News of the President's waking from his coma was powerful. World leaders who had only spoken to Porter or met him briefly were now concerned to find out if he was the same man he had been before being shot.

Vice President Sundee Ives, pock marked White House Chief of Staff Graham Newcome, and White House Comm Director, Cinnamon Higdon, all raced to Walter Reed in the middle of the night when they got the word. Porter was able to greet them all and endure the poking, flashlights in the eye, and easily a dozen cold stethoscopes of his team of doctors. Only Dr. Leonard Millhuff, who has been the President's doctor and had performed the procedures which had saved Porter's life, was absent. As fortune would have it, he was the star of a three day medical conference in California on major E.R. trauma practices. He was quickly on a special military flight within hours back to D.C.

The President's family was all there too, with kisses and double handed handshakes. The only news he could get from anyone was that he'd been shot, struck his head when he fell, and had been in a coma for just over two months. He knew there was more to tell, but he had to process that. He was promised stacks of newspapers and a detailed accounting of what he'd missed --- tomorrow.

When Porter found himself yawning, he told the Vice President, "You'd think I'd been sleeping long enough --- but that's not the way I feel."

"Please let the President get some rest," the Oriental attending physician, spoke for all to hear him.

The small crowd left and Porter closed his eyes. He opened them when he felt someone gently take his hand. It was Deidra putting her head down beside their intertwined fingers and softly kissing the back of his hand.

"Are we sleeping together now?" he asked with the small smile he could muster.

"We have been for some time now. You just haven't noticed. Besides, it's my shift. Sleep."

He did.

~

Across town at the Watergate complex, another group assembled in a paid for but rarely used suite.

Stylish and attractive Deliah Rome, former Director of White House Communication, stalked the carpet in a skirt opened up the side enough to display her sexy, well-toned legs. She knew she was being watched by the men in the room because to the thirty-five year old, sex was a weapon to be used freely.

The men, five in all, included other Leo Gibson staffers; portly, yet impeccably dressed former Presidential advisor and campaign manager, Willis Reiner sat across from a medium framed and thinning haired, former Assistant-Chief-of-Staff, Bryce Brooks. The other men were all political operatives steeped in D.C. politics and Democratic tactics.

"Is Victor coming or not?" Deliah demanded.

"I called him," Willis Reiner said, "but all I got was his voice mail."

Sixty-three-year-old Victor Chesterfield, Gibson's king maker and

White House Chief-of-Staff, had been a charter member of this group assembled by the bitter former Communications Director who was fired the day she returned to the White House by the new upstart President. While the completely bald, rimless spectacle wearing Chesterfield had been the organizational power behind the now dead President, it had always been the manipulative and scheming Deliah who was the subtle and devious heart of the Leo Gibson political force. Chesterfield had stayed on as Chief-of-Staff with the new President until after his State Of The Union address. It was that very night that Chesterfield had packed his office and left because he knew he could not control Porter Randall as he and Deliah had done with Gibson.

"We need him!" Deliah pounded her fists on the table.

"We all knew Randall would eventually wake up," Reiner said.

"Thank you for stating the obvious, Willis. The question is, what do we do now? We've lost all our people with real strength there."

"There's still the Attorney General," Bryce Brooks said running his hand through the remaining strands of his hair.

"Winchell Hardwick," Deliah spat, "is a spineless, sycophant. Why do you think we put that allergenic little shyster in that position? I wonder if Randall even knows Hardwick is even in his cabinet.

"No," she said turning away from the table and crossing to the window not seeing deep snow covering everything, "what we need is something for the reporters we control. When Randall woke up, we lost part of the front page and the A block on TV without our *'hero who saved the President.'* That's all page five if we're lucky and D block if the story doesn't disappear altogether."

"There is Randall's fitness to resume office," Willis Reiner offered with his thumbs in the vest pockets of his bulging belly.

Deliah whipped around wearing a wicked grin.

"That's what we need, Willis. He's been in a coma for two months. He can't just step right back into the Oval Office. What kind of peril would it put the whole world in to have someone not completely in command of his faculties with his finger on the button? Yes. Yes!"

"The world wants American leadership," Bryce added, "but not from the little lady from New Hampshire and certainly not a cowboy who might do something crazy at any moment."

"Let's run with that," she said. "Contact all your sources and get them to go there. I'll knock out a list of talking points and text it to you all --- on your burner phones."

"What about Congress?" Reiner asked. "Most of our people are keeping their heads down and their mouths shut. The public really bought into Randall's proposed amendments. Those on our gravy train are anxious."

"I'm still working on that. The polls are not in our favor. We been able to keep both measures isolated in different committees. The less said about them the better. Let's try to keep those amendments out of the spot light. "

CHAPTER 4

The President laughed as he read the top newspaper in his lap. He was trying to catch up with what had happened in the world since his being shot. He was on the third reporting of the incident citing the details of the attempted capture and arrest of the black clad figure fleeing the Milwaukee airport who shouted "Alah akbar!" He said nothing to the authorities but an ISIS flag was found in one of his pockets.

The story about the President's condition related a moment by moment account of what the Secret Service, Cinnamon Higdon, and the medical techs had done to get Porter from the floor of the hangar to the operating room on Air Force One.

"Did I really say that?" he asked as he chuckled and repeated the line, "'Thanks for giving me the finger.'"

In the spacious private hospital room where the President had been moved from I.C.U. after he had passed all the physician's original tests sat his sister, Irene, Deidra McAffie, and his Director of White House Communication. Cinnamon lowered her head and blinked as she confessed, "No, sir."

"It was my idea, Porter," Deidra said from beside his bed without any hesitation. "I remembered how Regan's quip about forgetting to duck helped after he had been shot. Seeing how the nation was reacting as I flew to get here, I thought a little levity might help."

"Well, it does sound like something I'd say," he laughed looking up at Deidra. Then to Cinnamon he said, "Good thinking on your part to put that out. It did help, I presume?"

"Yes, sir," Cinnamon said. "It was repeated on every news show, late night talk show and every paper in the country."

Porter chuckled again and turned the page.

"I get the feeling there's something I'm missing --- beside the two months," he said reaching for the next day's papers.

"You'll come to it," Irene said. "We think it's a good idea for you to catch up on things in order."

"You're probably right," he said and turned back to his reading.

There was a tap at the door.

"Come in," Porter said.

The door opened and in came hooked nose, grey haired General Lee Evans, Chairman of the Joint Chiefs, followed by squat, forty-year old Leigh Janda, official White House Photographer with his Nikon D4 digital clicking away. Three other military aids were also in tow.

"General," Porter said returning the smart salute of the uniformed four-star general.

Evans turned to one of his aids who held out and flipped open a flat metal box for the general.

"Mr. President, as Commander In Chief wounded in the course of performing his duty, I am empowered to award you this Purple Heart." The general took the award out of the purple velvet box and leaned down and pinned it above the pocket of the President's hospital gown. The general stepped back and turned to his other aid who offered a second award box. From it General Evans took a Silver Star.

Before the Chairman of the Joint Chiefs could even turn towards the President, Porter held up a hand in a *stop* motion.

"No, General! I'll accept the Purple Heart --- but no one deserves a metal for a speech --- unless it's Lincoln's Gettysburg Address or Martin Luther King's 'I Have A Dream' speech. If I accept this, the next thing you know speeches like Bill Clinton's 'I Did Not Have Sex With That Woman' and Nixon's 'I'm Am Not A Crook' will be called examples of American literature."

Porter held General Evan's intense blue eyes before the general put the metal back in the box and closed the lid.

All the while Leigh Janda kept clicking his camera and gathering images for history. The fringe of remaining blond hair around the edges of his head, were as mussed as always, but the man had an eye for picture no one could deny.

"Thank you, General," Porter said looking down at the Purple Heart. "You have just given me an idea. While I'm at Walter Reed, why don't you join me for a little exercise and we'll award metals to some deserving people right here?"

"Yes, sir," Evan's said with evident admiration in his voice. "Let me gather the names, awards, and locations --- and I'll be back."

The President extended his hand to the general who shook it firmly, did a smart about face and exited the room.

"Cinnamon," Porter said as the door hissed closed and Mr. Janda snapped a few more pictures, "I think you're going to have to have that display box behind my desk redone."

She opened her phone as she headed for the door, "I'm on it, Mr. President."

"And Mr. Janda," Porter said to the photographer, "neither these pictures nor any you take with General Evan's and myself awarding metals here are for publication. Copies are to go only to servicemen and women and their families."

"And the National Archives, Mr. President," Janda said in his raspy voice.

"All right --- but this is no photo op. Understood?"

"Yes, sir."

Porter went back to his reading as the photographer left with a quizzical look on his face.

When Deidra, Irene and Porter were alone, Deidra leaned down and kissed Porter on the cheek.

"What's that's for?" he asked.

"Just for being you," she said.

Irene was holding back tears of pride as his sister she could not restrain.

CHAPTER 5

"Are you professionally satisfied that your ol' man is still playing with a full deck?" Porter asked his six month pregnant daughter Page as they strolled the hospital hallways arm in arm, two Secret Service Agents less than a step behind.

"Professionally and personally," she said --- "if you can answer one question for me --- honestly."

"That sounds ominous. Ask --- notice I didn't say 'shoot.'"

Page smiled.

"Okay. Here it comes. Are you aware of how much Aunt Deidra loves you and just as importantly how much you love her?"

"What happened to my little girl? She would never have asked her father such things?"

"She grew up with loving parents, one of whom she's lost, and the other who was almost killed. I belive he has been suffering in silence long enough. I've always loved Aunt Deidra and Uncle Darren. I also know that Uncle Darren, as wonderful a surgeon as he was and as great business partner as he was to you — he couldn't keep it in his pants. I hate what he did to Aunt Deidra in their marriage and I believe --- eventually, he couldn't live with what he had become — at least partly because of what he was doing to her. I think, deep down, that's the reason he took his own life."

"There is more to it that that — but you certainly have grown up," Porter said a little surprised. "When did you figure all this out?"

"Years ago but it's been a long time coming in being able to openly admit it. It sounds like I didn't love Uncle Darren but I did. And so did Aunt Deidra."

They turned a corner and kept moving silently for a while.

"But she's suffered enough," she looked up at her father, "and you've mourned Mom enough. She would want more for you than this continued loneliness. You'll never forget her and neither will I, but --- you and Aunt Deidra have paid whatever price fate, destiny, or your own consciousness demands. You know how quickly this life can end. And I don't want anything more for both of you than what you deserve. You've stepped up to this job as President when you could have let it slide --- and you are where God wants you to be. But I don't believe He wants you to carry this burden alone."

"Again," he said stopping and facing Page, "where is my daughter and what have you done with her?"

"She's right here, Dad. Now, if you're playing with a full deck, I think it's time hearts trump anything else on the table."

Porter took Page in his arms and hugged her for what seemed like five minutes but the mutual embrace was really less than a one full minute.

When he released her, tears were running down both their faces.

"You didn't learn that kind of compassion and understanding so beyond your years from me or from school. I can only guess you got it from Mom."

They kissed each other on the cheek and continued their walk.

When they arrived back at his room, General Evans and four other officers, one from each service, and White House Photographer, Leigh Janda, awaited him. General Evans saluted and Porter returned the courtesy.

"Whenever you are ready, Mr. President, the general said, "we are prepared to make some rounds with you."

To his daughter, Porter said, "You and Kirk should really get back to Lubbock. I know your students miss you and it's about time for mid-terms."

"They won't be pleased that you remembered that, Dad. But you're right. We're flying out tonight."

Father and daughter kissed again before Porter turned to the military entourage.

"Let's get to it," Porter said to General Evans. He left with them, Leigh Janda, and President Randall's Secret Service detail. Porter was now dressed in standard issue Walter Reed hospital gown but wore a dark blue bathrobe with the gold Presidential emblem on the chest.

The group returned three hours later, exchanged salutes and the officers departed.

Inside the room an exhausted President Randall found the Vice President, his Director of White House Communication, Deidra, and his sister Irene waiting along with Chief-of-Staff Graham Newcome.

"Maybe this isn't the right time," Irene said as Porter crossed to the bed and sat, sweat evident on his forehead and his breath noticeably short.

"For what?" Porter managed to say.

"There is a crowd outside and all the networks. We were thinking you could step out the front door and say just a few words," Graham said looking around the room for other's reactions. Heads were nodding.

"Later," Cinnamon said.

"Obviously this isn't a good time." Vice President Ives said.

Porter held up his hand a moment but didn't speak. Deidra handed him three tissues from the box on his hospital table. Porter dabbed his forehead as Deidra popped the top on a can of cold Dr. Pepper beside the tissue. She handed it to him.

After he took a long drink, he looked up at Deidra and smiled.

"Thanks," he said.

"Mr. President," Sundee Ives began, "it won't look good if you're not ready."

"I'll be ready in a minute," Porter said.

"Are you sure?" the V.P. asked.

Porter nodded and took another swig of the soft drink.

Cinnamon handed the President two sheets of paper.

"These are notes from Therese." Theresa Herzog was the President's chief speech writer.

Porter quickly read the pages with his hazel eyes through gold-rimmed aviator bifocals.

"Good," he said handing the notes back to Cinnamon. His breathing was already back under control. "Let me hitch a ride down stairs in a wheel chair and then I'll get up and walk the last couple of steps."

"Mr. Yarbrough has everything set up," the V.P. said referring to Grant Yarbrough, the White House Press Secretary. "If you're sure, Mr. President."

"I'm sure," Porter said. Deidra pressed the call button and asked the nurse who answered to please bring a wheel chair to the President's room.

CHAPTER 6

Handsome White House Press Secretary, Grant Yarbrough, the son of a Vietnamese mother and a black father who had been an U.S. Air Force sergeant, was one of many holdovers from the Leo Gibson administration. The former CNN News anchor, had been almost apolitical if leaning somewhat left generally, had in the few months of working for Porter Randall, become surprisingly a solid fan of the new President. What he liked the most was that he was not asked to or expected to lie, cover up, or deflect direct questions from the media. Randall's first instruction to Yarbrough was to "play it straight." Unless there was something classified, Randall wanted his Press Secretary to be the person the reporters he faced everyday wanted to deal with.

One thing Grant had an eye for was good backdrops for photo opportunities or press conferences. It came from his years in TV news and it served him well now.

This abbreviated press conference was to be more of a photo op that also allowed President Randall the chance to say a very few words. The point was to show the injured and previously comatose President on his feet speaking as a way to illustrate that the man was on the mend and soon to be back in charge.

The site was the double doors on the ground floor of the iconic tower of the Walter Reed complex. There was plenty of room for the D.C. press corps on the wide snow shoveled sidewalks and even driveway. A cluster of microphones had been gathered in front of and around the lectern which had the medical facilities' crest displayed. Since Vice President Ives was still Acting President, Grant knew it was not appropriate to use the presidential seal.

Grant made sure to move the event away from the covered receiving concourse on the other side of the tower. While there was more room there, the Press Secretary had begun to think like his President, considering what was more important, a short message from the Commander-In-Chief or the daily work of Walter Reed. No one would know that Yarbrough had thought this through before making this call, but it wasn't something for which he now felt he needed acknowledgment. It was a new way of thinking --- but it felt right --- and good.

The President was rolled through the front doors and the nurse locked his chair in position while there was uncharacteristic cheering from the press. Porter stood and stepped to the lectern.

"Thank you," Porter said in a clear strong voice.

When the reporters and camera operators stopped their greeting, Porter looked around as he said, "I know I promised to have a news conference --- but, folks, this *ain't* it."

This garnered laughter from the media.

"I still owe you a full-fledged, open and honest conversation --- and it will happen --- soon. Today I am here to say only a few words, primarily --- to thank God for the chance to be here and do this --- and thank you to all the professionals, medical, security, pilots --- everyone who has had a hand in getting me this far.

"I want to specifically acknowledge the efforts of Acting President Sundee Ives. She accepted the job of Vice President knowing something like this was always a possibility --- but when the whole world actually does suddenly drop on your shoulders --- it's much more than you expected --- more, I'm sure, than she expected. At the same time I must compliment myself on my selection of Mrs. Ives. I don't think anyone would or could have handled these days in a more professional and steady way."

He turned to the Vice President dressed in a sheered lamb coat with the collar turned up again the wind.

"Thank you, Sundee," he said in voice that was filled with sincerity.

Turning back to the media Porter spoke into the microphones again.

"Believe me I'm surprised at the events that have occurred --- and I think by anyone's reckoning, I've used up all my sick leave and personal days for the year. If I don't get back to work soon, I'll have to take a cut in pay."

This comment delighted not just those bundled against the cold in front of the President but also the viewing public across the country because Porter had said in his very first televised address that he was going to do this job for only a dollar a year.

Porter read his audience well and waited for the right moment to continue.

"The events of the world while I've been napping are serious and require our best and proper response. So far the doctors here tell me I've suffered no brain damage due to either the shooting or the coma. When I've completely proven that I'm sound --- and regained my strength --- I'll return to my duties."

Porter paused a few moments and took a deep breath before he said, "I would like to stay here and talk to you longer --- and even answer a few questions --- but," he said gathering his hospital robe behind him in one hand, "I think someone's left the back door open."

This got the laugh he expected. Over it he said, "Thanks for coming. Please continue to pray for me and for the United States of America."

Porter walked back to his wheel chair and sat down. The nurse unlocked the wheels and turned him around as the President raised his hand in a wave.

CHAPTER 7

The next morning was spent with the neurologists, psychiatry and psychology specialists of the Walter Reed Medical Center. Doctor Millhuff, the Presidential Physician, was also in attendance and asked some probing questions along the way. By noon there was a unanimous agreement from the team that the President was emotionally, intellectually, and cognitively sound. Porter had a feeling that if Dr. Millhuff had been allowed a vote among the group there would have been at least one dissenting voice.

The President was watching the news when Dr. Millhuff reluctantly delivered the summary verdict. Porter didn't seem much interested in the medical verdict but was all but totally focused on the large screen TV mounted on the wall at an angle at the foot of his bed between the wall and ceiling.

Taking the official document from his physician, the President asked Millhuff, "Have you heard about this?"

Millhuff glanced at the screen and noted that it was news alert before he said with only a hint of repressed sarcasm, "I'm sorry, Mr. President, "but my focus has been elsewhere this morning."

"Then you need to stand here a minute and catch up."

The story was about twenty-two school busses across the nation which had been boarded by automatic weapons carrying men who sprayed the vehicles with gunfire. Video from one of the busses showed the ski-masked gunman walk down the aisle and point blank shoot any students left alive.

Even Millhuff was aghast at what he was seeing.

According to anchors and reporters, the busses seemed to be totally random and carried children from kinder to high school. The only good news was that on at least two occasions, armed bus drivers had killed the would-be perpetrators before they could get up the steps into the busses.

"Get me my clothes!" Porter demanded throwing back his covers and swinging to the side of his bed. He ripped off his hospital gown and was totally nude when Deidra handed him his boxer shorts followed by his socks. In a matter of moments President Randall was dressed.

Irene had gone to the door and told the Secret Service Agents Joe Lamb and Bryant Polaski to get the President a car --- any car. Immediately! He was going to the White House!

The day's total busses attacked were forty-six. One thousand, seven hundred sixty-two, students, drivers, teachers, and special ed workers had been killed. Only nine had survived long enough to get to the hospital. Three of those didn't make it and died of their wounds before physicians could save them. Just over a dozen attacks had been prevented by bus drivers or, in one case a homeowner who had used her own pistol to stop the masked attacker before he could board the bus.

Not since 9/11 had the nation suffered such a shock. Because this one involved so many children it was worse by a factor of five, one television psychologist had said in an often repeated interview clip.

In the White House Situation Room the weight was primarily on the F.B.I. as the nation's only national police force. Reports were funneled to the perpetually grim faced F.B.I. Director, Leon Nickleby. At sixty years old, Nickleby had broad shoulders, white blonde hair, piercing grey/green eyes. While every other man in the room, including the President, had loosened their ties, the F.B.I. Director remained as picture ready as if he'd just joined them from a professional make-up table.

"The nine year old girl in Parker, Colorado, will make it," he said hanging up his phone.

"ISIS is claiming credit on one of their websites," the grand ol' spy, Clancy Darren, the Director of National Intelligence, said keeping his phone to his ear. The weathered old man with a clarity to his wrinkled face spoke in his nasal high pitched voice. "There are celebrations in the streets of Iran."

Porter turned to his Chief-of-Staff, Graham Newcomb sitting in a chair near-by.

"I want to speak to a joint session of Congress tomorrow and national TV time tonight at nine o'clock our time."

"Yes, sir," Graham said headed for the door to make it happen.

Porter turned to Cinnamon Higdon on his other side. "Get Therese started on a declaration of war against Islamic terrorism --- no matter what they call themselves or where they are."

"I think I know what you want. I'll also get one of the other speech writers to work on the TV address."

"Use Kenny Fallen," Vice President Ives said touching Cinnamon's arm. "He'd be just the one for this."

Porter nodded and his Director of White House Communications left without another word.

To the F.B.I. Director the President said, "I think it's time to pull in anyone one high up on your terror list. In particular let's look at their rat holes like Dearborn, Michigan and up in Minnesota."

Leon Nickleby reached for his phone.

"I think we need to reach out to the Muslim community," his brother-in-law Mark Meekan, retired N.A.S.A. rocket scientist, and presidential advisor said. "This will give them the chance to get onboard and really do something beyond talk.

"Some of the children killed were Muslim," Nickleby said with his hand over the mouth piece of his phone.

"I want some facts on that. I'd like to include it in what I say tonight."

"Yes, sir." Nickleby returned to his phone.

By nine P.M. Eastern, the cameras, teleprompters, and microphones were set up in the Oval Office. Porter was making notes on his copy of the remarks in front of him up until the moment the red light on the main camera lit up.

CHAPTER 8

"No President ever wants to address this nation about what I've come to talk to you about tonight," Porter began. As Cinnamon Higdon would tell him later, he should have napped before the speech. He looked gaunt, haggard, and wrung out --- but it was the way most of the American public was feeling this night.

"The past twenty-four hours will be remembered for the mindless, cruel, and barbaric slaughter of innocence. Those who have claimed the faith of Islam as their reason and their justification for the murder of children have unmasked themselves before the world --- we all now see them for who and what they are. These are not the acts of faith or morality. Instead it was a carefully thought through, minutely planned, scheduled, and deliberately painful act of terrorism aimed at our hearts through our children.

"For anyone who ever doubted the intent or the reason behind this international cancer, the diagnosis is now crystal clear. The black flag they currently rally around is an appropriate reflection of the soul of this movement. It is a black hole, consuming everything in its grasp and reaching out for more."

The President paused and bit his bottom lip before he proceeded.

"It must be called out for what it is --- not a faith, not even a corruption of a faith ---although it wishes to cling to that false claim. This is a political movement of greed and ambition; a thirst for power and world domination --- distorted in its vision and its aims. The final goal of this malignancy is the absolute control of the lives of every living person in the world --- to suppress women --- to torture children and the weak --- to wallow in ignorance --- and to butcher any who dare to disagree with any of its twisted concepts. This threat is not unlike the surges of slavery, colonialism, Communism, Nazism, Fascism --- and an evil list of ethnic and racial purity movements throughout the dark side of humankind's history. Islamic extremism --- under the name and flags of ISIS, al-Qaeda, Al-Shabaab, the Army of Islam, Koko Haram, Hamas, Hezbollah, Islamic Jihad, the Taliban --- and a multitude of self-proclaimed fronts, and liberation movements --- are today's common malevolence."

For a moment Porter closed his eyes, swallowed and then looked up at the camera again as he continued.

"There are common attributes these fanatics share and it is time to realistically face up to these factors and --- yes --- profile accordingly.

"But let us do it carefully with justice and honor.

"For us as a nation and a culture these will be difficult days as we must both be aware of our words and our deeds. We must not resort to bigotry and broad accusations without proof. Like the wise and courageous people of Charleston, South Carolina, whose reaction after the senseless murder of some of their citizens inside a church, we must react with love, and compassion first so that other innocents are not harmed in a backlash. As you must know, there were Muslim children murdered along with all the others today. There are Muslim families hurting as much as any tonight.

"Remember, too, there are cultural and religious Muslims who have come to America to escape the brutality and savagery of those who have gained power and even dominance in their own homelands and places of worship. But Muslims who are against these extremists must demonstrate through words and actions that they, too, stand against the wicked jihad they have allowed to silence them for so long. With physical and moral courage, those who want to live in peace must rise now and be counted. If you will not stand with us, your silence means you agree with these monsters and what they want. It also means you want to live under that kind of repression, domination, and cruelty. If that is not your desire --- this --- today --- and in the days of this conflict to come are the days to exhibit your true colors. It is time for you to be Americans first --- and stand beside those of *all* other faiths to ensure that we remain the land of the free and the home of the brave.

"The American giant has been awoken and cost to those who have attacked us will be great, indeed. Let there be no doubt about that in anyone's mind.

"Tomorrow I will address a joint session of Congress calling for a declaration of war against the forces of terrorism --- in whatever form --- in whatever part of the world they hide. It has become our lot to be the generation who takes on this massive foul beast which has been allowed to grow and mastasize. Like our fathers and forefathers, we will answer this call with righteous fury and overwhelming might against this evil --- as they have done in the past. There are no sacrifices too great --- no demands too large for us to meet this malicious demon ---wherever it goes, wherever it hides, or wherever it seeks shelter.

Porter took a depth breath and narrowed his tired eyes and he pressed on.

"It is not vengeance we will exact --- because vengeance is not ours --- and we do not want it to return on us. But we know profoundly what has been so inhumanly taken from us. Therefore we will seek justice --- total and unequivocal justice --- in the hearts and souls of those who have been shattered today --- but also in the records of history.

"No one will be allowed to deprive us of our lives, our children, our liberties, or our paths to happiness through unbridled violence and hatred. Anyone who will stand with us --- we welcome your help --- for those who will oppose us --- not even the devil will sustain you against us.

"In the days to come, be sure to honor the memory of those we have lost in everything you do. We have already begun to prepare to unleash the powers of the upright and the strength of the virtuous in the name of the innocent.

"Please pray for the families and communities in so much pain tonight --- and pray for yourself --- for the strength and endurance we will need. But also please pray for me --- and for The United States of America.

"Good night and God bless us all."

CHAPTER 9

To the hushed joint session of Congress Porter said most of what he had conveyed to the American public the night before. But he was emphatic as he spoke to the two houses of the Legislative Branch. There had been scattered clapping but mostly the elected officials sat and listened having spent the previous twenty-four hours hearing from their constituents. They unquestioningly knew what they had to do.

"This cannot and must not be a war run by politicians," President Randall said, "either from the White House or from these very halls. I will set out a strategy in broad strokes with the help of the Pentagon and then I will ask for your support. But I ask you not to attempt to tie the hands of those who will be placing their lives on the line. We have seen the disastrous results of such policies from Korea, to Vietnam, to Iraq and Afghanistan.

"Our great grandfathers thought they were fighting the war to end all wars. It is time to face up to the fact that armed conflicts have always been a part of human history and will forever be so --- *as much as we would love to have it differently*. Sociopaths and psychopaths, insane fanatics and mere deluded individuals will rise to power and threaten both their nearest neighbors and even the whole world.

"British philosopher Edmund Burke correctly pointed out, 'The only thing necessary for the triumph of evil is that good men do nothing.' But sometimes there is a greater danger than doing nothing --- the peril is in taking only half measures --- not completing the task once it is undertaken. Don't allow posterity the need to *continue* much less *repeat* what we have only had the guts to begin.

"Clearly this business is an undertaking we have not sought but which has been thrust upon us. But let us accept our ration of history with the courage and resolve of our forefathers who took up arms against other iniquities --- and even those who came here to escape such a fate elsewhere --- only to learn the sad but significant oxymoronic truth that it is only by standing and fighting that can freedom, dignity --- and even peace be achieved and preserved."

The President scanned the chamber and turned to look up at the words "In God We Trust" chiseled into the marble above and behind him before he again faced his audience.

"I stand here today asking for a clear and unambivalent call to arms --- a Declaration of War against Islamic terrorism in all its forms, all its names, and wherever on God's earth they exist --- at home and overseas!"

All but a very few members of both houses took to their feet and gave full and enthusiastic applause and vocal approval of what their Commander-In-Chief had said.

Porter let the applause continue until it was done and members had taken their seats again.

"I come asking this in the name of the American people --- and asking that you take this action with the cold, clear, knowledge that even your sons and daughters --- your grandchildren --- your nieces and nephews may be the ones called upon to man the guns, fly the planes, and sail the ships into harm's way. This is to be no rich man's war and poor man's fight. If we dare to take this step --- we must all be in it together.

"I now go to pray for you in this hour of consequential decision. May God have mercy on us all. Please pray for me --- and pray for the United States of America."

With those words Porter stepped down and left the legislative hall with the members all getting to their feet silently knowing what was before them.

Deidra, Irene and her husband, Mark, waited outside the capital building. When Porter jointed them, they were driven to 13113 New York Avenue N.W., less than two blocks from the White House --- the New York Avenue Presbyterian Church. Although it was Wednesday, the church was almost full.

Porter lead the way down the main aisle of cherry wood pews to the President's pew where Presidents Adams, Jackson, and Lincoln, both Harrisons, William Henry and Benjamin, Polk, Pierce, Buchanan, Andrew Johnson, Eisenhower, and Nixon had sat. The organ played hymns and worshipers came and went.

After half an hour Porter and his party left. Petitioners waited outside, silently and the Presidential party emerged. There were no cheers or applause --- but a few "God bless you, Mr. President" were softly spoken from the crowd.

Back at the White House the President had a Congressional Declaration of War on his desk by four P.M. He also got the formal paper signed by the Senate's President Pro Tem, the Speaker of the House, and the Vice President officially restoring Porter to office as President. At this point it was a mere formality but something that needed to happen. He spent the rest of the day on secure video phone discussing the next step forward to other world leaders.

The last task of the day was to request his medical records from Walter Reed. Porter didn't understand how he had survived what should have been a kill shot and two months in a coma. He wanted to see in black and white --- even the video --- of what he had been through.

Thursday a Conference on Islamic Terrorism was announced for the following Monday in Brussels.

Following doctors' orders, Porter rested as much as he could while his staff and the Pentagon set to work on a coherent strategy for the coming conflict. Deidra left on Friday to fly back to Amarillo. Porter had never felt so alone or so inadequate to his job or the future of the world.

CHAPTER 10

The Islamic Terrorism Conference took place at N.A.T.O. headquarters in Haren, an outlying part of the city of Brussels, capitol of the once Dutch colony established in 580 A.D. Today Belgium was a duel language nation, officially both Dutch and French. For the last couple of hundred years French had been the language in the south and Dutch in the north; even the road signs reflected both languages. But in reality, the working language today was French.

Brussels was, for all practical purposes, also the capital of what parts of the European Union continued to function. This union was a trading and economic creation meant to mimic the United States by uniting independent countries like our states for financial and commercial exchange. However the central authority kept wanting to acquire more and more power, not unlike the federal government in the U.S. In the U.S. the central government had little by little stripped away many of the powers and privileges of the independent democratic experiments of the states that the creators of the Constitution had envisioned. This fact seemed to have either escaped or been purposely ignored by those who proposed the E.U. in 1993. But unlike the states in the U.S. union, the sovereign nations of the European

Union refused to yield their individualism and their rights to a bumbling, insensitive central authority. Thus the faltering E.U. continued as an inundated corruption, largely distrusted and inept.

Second only to mystery writer Agatha Christi's character, dapper and idiosyncratic post World War I Belgium detective, Hercule Poirot, N.A.TO. was the nation's best known creation. Formed from the 1949 North Atlantic Treaty, the organization was the integrated defense system of North America and Western Europe. It was the Korean War of the 1950's that stiffened the resolve of its members to stand together against the Warsaw Pact nations of the Soviet bloc in 1955.

Its biggest challenge came, surprisingly from within. France, in 1966 under President Charles De Gaulle, wanted more power and French influence in N.A.T.O. When the U.S. and Great Britain, under U.S. President Eisenhower and U.K. Prime Minister Harold Macmillan, refused to bow to the ego driven leader, France withdrew and formed its own defenses against the Soviets.

France pulled both its Atlantic and Channel fleets from N.A.T.O. At the height of the crisis, De Gaulle demanded all non-French N.A.T.O. troops out of France. Dean Rusk, then U.S. Secretary of State was quoted as asking de Gaulle whether his order included "the bodies of American soldiers in France's cemeteries?"

The 1991 ending of the Warsaw Pact, as a part of the reforms lead by Soviet leader Mikhail Gorbachev, precipitated the end of the Cold War. The tearing down of the Berlin Wall, and the reuniting of East and West Germany, lead to reorganization of N.A.T.O. and in 2009 France's full return to the organization.

In 1997, N.A.T.O. began conducting a significant downsizing of its command structure to twenty headquarters from its previous sixty-five. June of 2003 saw further changes as N.A.T.O.'s military command, HQ for the Supreme Allied Commander – Atlantic, was replaced by a new command established in Norfolk, Virginia, and SHAPE, (Supreme Headquarters Allied Powers Europe) became the headquarters of the new Allied Command Operations.

Russian presidents Vladimir Putin, Dmitry Medvedev and then

Putin again, had strong objections to the proposed Ukrainian and Georgian membership in N.A.T.O. The Russian leaders also objected to the missile defense system for Poland and the Czech Republic.

In one of his many backwards steps, President Barack Obama in 2009 suggested instead the use of the ship based Aegis System. N.A.T.O. was able to keep its status quo in its nuclear deterrent for Europe by upgrading the targeting capabilities of the B-61nuclear bombs (0.3 to 340 kilotons) still on station and additionally deploying the weapon on the stealthier Joint Strike Fighter. The crisis of Russian invasion of Crimea in 2014 moved N.A.T.O. to form spearhead forces of 5,000 at bases in Estonia, Lithuania, Latvia, Poland, Romania, and Bulgaria.

All of this had become working knowledge to President Randall by the time he stepped off of Air Force One for the N.A.T.O. conference. He also knew the biggest threat facing the world was lack of American leadership beginning with Obama. Leo Gibson's administration had carried the same torch to the rear of every crisis and when Porter arrived at N.A.T.O., he knew he might well be viewed as the leader of a now spineless U.S.

Porter was shocked when he entered the blue carpeted conference hall and walked to his chair in front of the assembled flags of member nations as the entire assembly came to its feet clapping. They all knew about the attempted assassination on the American President's life, his long coma and meticulous recovery. But they had also seen his addresses to the American public and to the joint session of Congress calling for a Declaration of War. To many, these were signs of the American leadership Europe knew in the dark days of World War II and Korea --- but rarely since.

The President made his way around the circle of desks shaking hands of many he did not know, and acknowledging some faces he had only known over the video of international calls. There was an international compass insignia woven into the center of the carpet and one prong pointed clearly toward the area of the table where Porter took his seat.

THE RELUCTANT INCUMBENT

When Porter reached his seat, he shook hands with U.S. N.A.T.O. Ambassador Garth Upson. Porter had spoken by phone with Upson both before he left D.C. and in route from Air Force One. Silver haired with heavy lidded eyes, the seventy year old Ambassador was a billionaire businessman, who ran a family centered mail order and Internet catalogue corporation. A Princeton graduate, he had been selected for the draft by lottery during Vietnam where he served as a helicopter pilot. After his service he went to graduate school in political science and had become a confirmed liberal. But instead of pursuing a career in politics, he went back into family business which he soon ran and improved into the vastly successful business it was today.

Upson managed to publish two books on Vietnam expressing the view that everything about the war, including his actions, were not only wrong but verged on criminal. He became a darling of what was left of the old anti-war movement. He got involved in national politics as a donor and was a significant contributor to the campaigns of the former President, Leo Gibson.

It always looked as if Upson was about to smile. This and his affability had brought him to the attention on Gibson's team when it was picking ambassadors. Due to his former military background it seemed a natural fit to put him in as the United States Permanent Representative to N.A.T.O. with the rank of full ambassador.

Upson and his trophy third wife enjoyed the life in Europe. He was completely at ease with the lack of leadership his President demanded of him. He was often put out with the upper echelon who served him at N.A.T.O. because they were much more hawkish than he was, but the power was his and he gladly, like Leo Gibson, lead from behind --- but only then when absolutely necessary.

Ambassador Upson had never experienced the pressure he had since the death of Leo Gibson. He had seen, heard, and read about the new accidental President and did not like in the least this man's approach to government and leadership. He was surprised at how much his wife was taken by Porter and had to agree that the man had a certain charm, but Upson didn't sign on to be a wartime figurer in any sense. He would never have even used the words *Islamic* or *Muslim* in conjunction with terrorism. Thus he was more than happy to let President Randall do the speaking at the emergency council on Islamic Terrorism when other countries yielded their right to speak to the Americans.

"This war has been a long time coming," Porter said without consulting his notes but glancing around the circular desks of powerful leaders. "It is not a crusade and it is not a holy war --- but it is a war against exactly that. Let us call this multi-continent fight what it truly is --- World War III. It will not be quick and it will not be easy. There have already been victims of this conflict and heroes of it as well.

"We are fighting a twisted ideal --- a cruel and heartless evil hiding behind and getting support from one of the major religions of our world. But make no mistake --- not all cultures nor all religions are morally equal.

"I am a Christian. The Great Commission of my faith tells me to 'Go therefore and make disciples of all the nations, baptizing them in the name of the Father and the Son and the Holy Spirit.' It is a command to spread the words of peace and love to all mankind. It does not demand that I murder, rape, and destroy any who do not accept the sacrifices made for them.

"It commands me that, 'If anyone will not welcome you or listen to your words, leave that home or town and shake the dust off your feet.' --- Move on in peace."

Porter looked down at his speech before he went on.

"The malevolence we face today has no such mission or desire --- just as in the last World War we faced foes who believed in their hearts that they were a superior race, culture, and had a God given right to rule the world in tyranny --- unrestrained by law --- or constitution --- or human rights.

"In 1785 two of my forefathers, Thomas Jefferson and John Adams, tried to negotiate with the envoy of the Muslim Barbary pirates. When asked what gave these pirates the right "...to make war upon nations who had done them no injury," --- the representative from Tripoli replied ...."

Porter read this to make sure he got it right.

"'It is written in our Quran, that all nations which had not acknowledged the Prophet were sinners, whom it was the *right* and *duty* of the faithful to plunder and enslave.'"

"Today's jihad includes beheadings, mass murder, and the mandatory imposition of sharia law throughout the world under an Islamic caliphate of the design of the terrorists who call themselves *the faithful*.

"For fourteen centuries jihad has left a path of conflict and untold human suffering. Tens of thousands of women and children have been enslaved, forced to convert to Islam --- and even then they suffered ritual gang-rapes, genital mutilations and lives of sexual slavery. Jihadists have sent innocent people on forced marches, put them to hard labor, and beaten them --- many to the point of death.

"These jihadists have no moral or religious obligation to keep faith with their words or treaties to anyone they consider *infidels*."

Porter took a drink of water and let his words sink in before he went on.

"Thank God not every Muslim is inclined or obligated to take part in this cruelty called jihad --- but too many have remained silent and not opposed it either. The unfortunate truth is that only an overwhelming force of arms will end this rage of hate --- and it must be ended in total and unconditional defeat. Then perhaps those Muslims with love and tolerance in their hearts will find a voice and truly begin the labor of dealing with their faith as members of a worldwide movement to heal Islam from within."

Applause washed over the conference hall and the representatives of other N.A.T.O. nations.

"And a final caution --- this must be said. As we take on this task, we must stay aware of both Russia and China. These nations have territorial and political ambitions of their own. We should not expect any assistance in battling this Islamic Terrorist scourge from either of these nations. In fact, we can expect one or both to attempt to take advantage of our fight to advance their own interests at the expense of the whole world. We must stay alert."

Everyone in the hall stood in unison to support the President's call for war. It was now time for him to layout his strategy.

CHAPTER 11

Garth Upson, U.S. N.A.T.O. Ambassador, who was sitting beside President Randall was not at all pleased with the forthright, dynamic, and plain language he was hearing from his new boss. He was deciding how best to resign his position. This coming war, World War III as the President had said in no uncertain terms, was not at all what Upson had signed on for. He wanted the title and prestige of an ambassador, but he had been running from war and its consequence ever since Vietnam. How could he remain in a post which was going to demand leadership into worldwide conflict?

When the representatives of the other N.A.T.O. nations had taken their seats again, Porter spoke once more.

"It is sad that we have come to this. It would have been much easier, more diplomatic, and cheaper in blood, lives, and resources for those before us to have dealt with this problem --- but since it has become our charge, our calling, and our obligation --- let us pick up this torch and keep it high until the ultimate victory is won. Our children and future generations must know us for our willingness and courage to do what no one wanted to do --- but which history has put in our path.

"Specifically, this is what we, The United States of America, propose. Three simple yet ultimately demanding and costly steps.

"One: with overwhelming force and the determination to see it to the very end, seek out our enemy in every city, town, village, basement, cave and rat hole where they may hide --- and exterminate their contamination in both the real world but also on-line over the Internet.

"We must acknowledge at the beginning that this will be a nasty --- and, yes, cruel --- war. The cowards we face have already proven they have no regard for the innocent, for women or children. Thus when they take shelter in schools, hospitals and even mosques, they must be rooted out --- at high and regrettable human costs. But this will be necessary because those with whom they live and who have given them aid and assistance in the past will become now their human shields. We would wish that it were not so --- but we have to understand it will be --- and our only choices will be bad ones. When we are judged by God and by history we must be on our knees openly admitting the wrongs that we will have had to choose. All we can do is the best we can do. In the end if we are right --- to paraphrase Abraham Lincoln, what is said against us won't amount to anything. If the end brings us out wrong, then ten angels swearing we were right will make no difference."

The hall was totally silent. No world leader had ever said what Porter had and it was uncomfortable to hear --- but it was the honest and unvarnished truth with no wiggle room.

Porter breathed a few times before moving on.

"Secondly, when the time is right, we must redraw the maps of what we know as the Mid-east to not only insure the home of Israel but to also make a sovereign space for the Kurds --- and then do the same for the Sunnis, and the Shiites. These Muslim divisions have always chosen war over any other solution to their theological differences. We cannot and should not interfere. But neither should we squander our blood in what has been one of the worlds' longest and most futile reasons for hatred. Kingdoms in the Mid-east at peace should be allowed to continue in peace, but waring neighbors living in artificially created nation states must be given clear territory of their own. This step we propose be taken with the input of all parties involved and it is not one that will come easily.

"And lastly, we must find a way to encourage those of the true Islamic faith to discover their leaders who see the world as it is both today and in the future. Perhaps there will be Muslim Martin Luthers --- but this step is one Islam must take itself --- or what we begin today will have to all be done again and again by other generations to come.

"We, The United States of America, have chosen our path. We ask for N.A.T.O.'s backing and assistance --- because you, too, have suffered at the hands of this incarnate evil. Whatever path we choose as N.A.T.O. let us do so with clear heads and clean hearts --- asking for neither land, nor concessions, but only peace.

After a moment's pause, Porter added, "May God have mercy on us all."

There was no doubt about the backing of N.A.T.O. as once more the national leaders, ambassadors, generals, and aids all took to their feet responding with full throated support for the President's words.

CHAPTER 12

On the flight back to Washington Porter had some policy discussions with his thirty-one year old Chief-of-Staff, pock marked faced Graham Newcome, brother-in-law and Presidential advisor, Mark Meehan, and Sec. of Defense, Shepherd Claxton. They agreed that the N.A.T.O. conference had gone even better than anyone could have imagined.

Claxton, a left over political appointee from Leo Gibson's administration, was like Ambassador Garth Upson a less than enthusiastic supporter of the war efforts. The bony, hollow chested Claxton had been in the limo when Ambassador Upson had attempted to resign. He knew he was likely to meet with the same reaction if he, too, tried to quit. With no military background himself, the Secretary of Defense had felt out of place from the day he entered the Pentagon. He was a career politician and understood his role for then President Gibson was to keep the military in check as he had kept Democratic party members in line over the years.

Unfortunately there was no denying the fever for war after the bus terrorism. Claxton felt caught up in the tide and was completely out of his depths when the new President called for war and the mood in the Pentagon had seen a sudden shift of power in their direction. His decision had been to get out but now that seemed to be an impossibility. To be seen as abandoning his post in a time of war would be political suicide. Going along was all Claxton felt he could do. He would maintain his position and let the Generals run the place as they seemed to want to do from the beginning.

When the President adjourned the meeting, he picked up his phone and contacted his White House Communications Director to get an update of all things political in his absence. Cinnamon Higdon told the President about the embarrassing anti-war demonstrations which the usual suspects tried to organize. Dismal turnout was evident in the coverage from all the media. This, coupled with European enthusiasm for America's leadership under President Randall and the sound bites from his remarks in the N.A.T.O. conference, had bolstered Porter's support around the world. Only China and Russia were pushing back but their reactions weren't well received.

The unexpected news was a phone call Cinnamon had received from Porter's original Chief-of-Staff, Victor Chesterfield. The bald, rimless spectacles wearing, intelligent and savvy winner of the Congressional Medal of Honor in Vietnam had stayed in the White House Chief-of-Staff position as Porter had requested during the transition of the new President until Porter's State Of The Nation Address to Congress. The next morning Porter had found Chesterfield packing boxes and on his way out. In a no holds barred conversation, the former iron willed and king maker behind the Gibson administration had laid out specifically and pointedly exactly why the new President was naïve and unsuited for the high office he held by sheer accident. The new message he had delivered to Cinnamon on her private cell phone was that Chesterfield wanted a meeting with President Randall.

"That is a surprise," Porter said. "Did he say when?"

"A.S.A.P."

"Sure. Put him on the schedule and tell him to come on in."

"That's the problem. He doesn't want to meet you in the White House and he wants the meeting to be secret."

"Curioser and curioser. Victor doesn't do anything without a plan. So, what's his?"

"He'd like to meet you in Blair House. He wants to use a back entrance."

Blair House was off the corner of Lafayette Park which was directly across Pennsylvania Avenue from the White House. It was the official residence for Presidential guests and sat opposite the Eisenhower Executive Office Building west of the White House.

"Anything else?"

"He asked not to be on the schedule."

"He did. Victor is certainly covering his ass on this."

"I was thinking the same thing, Mr. President," Cinnamon said.

"Okay, let me get a good night's sleep first," Porter said rubbing the ache in his chest where the attempted assassin's bullet had entered his body. "Pencil in an hour and a half personal time for me on Tuesday. Let's say nine A.M. I'll use the underground passage to Blair House. Nobody will miss me."

"I'll make sure they don't."

"Is that it?"

"Just a suggestion," Cinnamon said.

"Tell me."

"How long has it been since you've called Deidra McAffie?"

Porter had to laugh.

"Yes, Mother," he said. "Or are you masquerading as cupid."

"More of the latter than the former," his beautiful aid told him sincerely. "You have a lot on your plate but you can't forget what's really important in your life. There's an open, round trip, first class ticket in Deidra's name at the Amarillo airport."

"On who's credit card?"

"Ah --- I'll have to look." From Cinnamon's end of the line Porter heard a rustling of paper. "Some doctor in Lubbock, I think. 'Can't seem to find the name."

"You've been taking to Page, haven't you?"

"Well, girls will talk."

"Yeah. That's what I thought," he smiled. "I'm calling Deidra now."

"Just remember, it's in the middle of the night in Texas."
"Yes, Mother."
They both clicked off.
Porter dialed and Deidra didn't sound sleepy in the least.
"Were you expecting me to call?" he asked.
"Not expecting exactly. Let's say --- hoping. I was doing some light reading. One of my favorite books."
"Do tell."
"It keeps me entertained and I love the unexpected humor. The sex isn't bad either."
"And the title?"
"<u>First Do No Killing</u>. It's a medical thriller."
It was Porter's first novel and a best seller. Currently it was being turned into a screenplay for production in Hollywood later in the year.
"'No piece of literature' if the critics are to be believed," he said.
"Screw the critics. I never like what they like. But I do know what I like."
"How would you like to spend a couple of days at Camp David? The Presidential retreat."
"Are you serious?"
"It would have to be a working and relaxing weekend."
"What are the amenities like? You know I'm a difficult woman to please."
"It's no Panhandle ranch house, but bedrooms are close to each other and privacy is guaranteed."
"You had me at bedrooms."

CHAPTER 13

The meeting in Blair House with Victor Chesterfield was a complete surprise to Porter beyond knowing his former Chief-Of-Staff wanted a very private meeting. Even the agenda of the meeting was a blank.

When Porter emerged into what looked from the outside to be a separate residence, he was still officially in Blair House but technically in Trowbridge House, an adjacent townhouse.

The structure was originally constructed by an engineer and mathematics professor, William Trowbridge, in 1859. It had several tenants over the years but currently it had been renovated and serves as an official guest residence for former U.S. presidents while in the capital.

Victor Chesterfield removed the empty bulldog pipe he used to smoke but now just chewed on as if it were a cigar when Porter joined him in one of the sitting rooms.

"Mr. President," the alert, bald sixty-three year old said as he stood.

Porter offered his hand and the Metal of Honor Winner shook it with a firm grip.

"We have an hour and a half," Porter said. "Let's sit."

They each took a wing backed leather arm chair near a burning fireplace.

"Thank you for seeing me, sir," Victor began.

"Victor, let's get back on a first name basis, okay? I was surprised to hear from you much less have you ask for a meeting after our last conversation."

"I don't regret anything I said."

"Nor do I. You were honest and blunt with me at a time that I really needed it."

"Things have changed as you must realize. You have earned yourself not just a constituency but the support and admiration of the nation --- and if the media reads it correctly --- and I'm never sure that they do --- you have the support of entire free world. I didn't see it at the time, but, Porter, you are the right man for this job at the right time."

"Thank you for saying that, Victor, but we both know you didn't come here to blow smoke up my skirt."

"No, sir, I didn't." Victor took a deep breath and said, "There are some powerful people who not only wish you ill, but I think might be behind the attempt to kill you. It'll never be proven, but I know these people exist. In the beginning I was a part of their conversations but when I began to suspect it was more than dirty tricks and politics, I left. They thought I was going to be their spy inside the White House. I don't spy for anyone."

"I have no doubt."

The two men sat looking at each other for a moment before Porter spoke once more.

"I presume it's the presence of these people who prompted your quick exit from the White House."

"Yes, sir. I had done what I had agreed to, but if I stayed any longer, whether or not I was a part of this --- conspiracy --- I would be culpable in my own mind for whatever they did in the future. When you were shot, I knew they had orchestrated it. I felt like I had left one of my own men behind in a war."

"Which is a guilt you still carry from your time as a Marine --- every time you see your Metal of Honor on your wall."

"They try to tell me it's survivor's guilt --- maybe that's part of it --- but this thing with you --- it goes way beyond anything so easily explained away."

"Believe it or not, I understand. Victor, when I walked away from my tours of duty I kept my metals in the footlocker I brought home and I never opened them."

"Do you want to know who I'm talking about in this --- conspiracy?"

"No. I don't want to get hung up on trying to get even with people who --- there are too many other things I need to focus on. Of course, you should have a frank conversation with the F.B.I. and the C.I.A. --- but leave me out of that loop. There's nothing constructive I can do about it. Let's set up a meeting with Leon Nickleby and Clancy Darren. In my mind they can be trusted to do what needs to be done without my input."

Victor Chesterfield was dumbfounded. How could this man not want revenge?

"I don't think I understand you, Porter. I guess I never have."

"There's a whole Congress up on the hill that mostly feel the same way."

"Not as many as you think, Mr. President. You have more support there than you know."

"We'll see after the special election." Porter was talking about the election called in over fourteen states to recall their members of Congress --- an election based on Porter's State Of The Union remarks.

Victor got to his feet.

"I'll speak to the F.B.I. and C.I.A. directors --- today. Thank you for hearing me out."

"Not so fast," Porter said not taking Victor's offered hand. "Sit down and talk to me about something else.

This time it was Victor who was in the dark. He slowly lowered himself into the bradded and tufted chair.

"Can you give me your opinion of Winchell Hardwick and Shepherd Claxton?"

"My *honest* opinion?"

"Are you capable of giving anything else?" the President asked already knowing the answer.

Victor sat back in his chair and put his pipe back in his mouth.

"Both were appointed because they were and always have been in Leo Gibson's pocket. They would have also fallen on their swords for Leo --- reluctantly but obediently --- expecting significant back end rewards for their sacrifices. Neither one is qualified for their jobs. Winchell does have a law degree but he's no lawyer and certainly isn't out for justice. As Attorney General his chief job was to be Leo's head witch hunter --- ready, willing, and unscrupulously prepared to bring the force of the whole government down on anyone Leo pointed out. If you replaced him with a vacancy, the American public might soon have faith in the Department of Justice again."

Victor thought a moment before he said, "Shepard Claxton still doesn't know the difference between a P.F.C. and a lieutenant commander --- and he doesn't care to learn. He's a joke in the Pentagon. We've never had a Defense Secretary who was less qualified. But then Leo never planned on an armed conflict with anyone. He always thought he could charm his way out of anything --- just like Obama. If I were you, I'd replace him with your National Security Advisor, Grace Spurlock. That would also give you a Hispanic in high places which your administration could use."

Porter nodded his head slowly.

"I agree with you on both counts --- but --- I'd rather have you as Secretary of Defense."

"Me? After what I've just told you?"

"Partly because you did tell me. Grace Spurlock would do a great job, but she's never been in uniform much less been under fire. She is a magnificent National Security Advisor. I want her judgement very close to me. I'd also like Victor Chesterfield as my Secretary of Defense."

CHAPTER 14

Shepard Claxton was allowed to handle his dismissal as he pleased --- within the next twenty-four hours. His choice was a 4:55 Washington time announcement that he was resigning effective immediately. His reasons were stated as "profound ideological differences" with the current administration over its aggressive war policy."

The wording was pure Delilah Rome, the first of Leo Gibson's inner circle Porter fired when he assumed the Presidency. The attractive but deeply vindictive Ms. Rome spent the night in hiding, working on background information for Claxton to make him sound informed and pure of heart — things he certainly was not. She laid out a series of talking points for him and gave him hell until he could recite them verbatim. The hollow chested, red rimmed blue eyed politician was also given detailed instructions on how to sit up and lean forward when he faced the cameras and reporters on every available outlet except Fox, which was denied any access to Claxton.

The far left, complete anti-war crowd rallied around the former Defense Secretary as if he was some sort of brave, guiding light of principal. When reporters pressed him about the recent terrorist attacks on American school children, Claxton was always, thanks to Delilah Rome's preparation, able to side step back to his talking points. His key sound bite was the Benjamin Franklin quote, "There never was a good war or a bad peace."

The White House response was that the decision to leave was Claxton's --- who was given the choice of resigning or being publically fired. In reaction to the Ben Franklin reference, handsome Press Secretary Grant Yarbrough said, "What we have been living in for the past dozen years was not peace but a one sided, openly declared war --- a war the west has tried to avoid with every possible tactic except resolve, determination, and strength. This *is* a bad war --- but it is not of our making. A peace which cost us so many children was not a *good* peace --- in fact, it was no peace at all. We are now facing up to that. Mr. Claxton and those who share his opinion may not help us in this war, but they will certainly enjoy the protection of those who will fight it --- and they will happily enjoy the ultimate real peace it will bring."

Before the President left for Camp David, he announced his pick for the next Secretary of Defense --- Victor Chesterfield. The press release was greeted with shock and dismay. Even members of the Senate who were clearly opposed to Porter had difficulty denouncing their former colleague and a Metal of Honor Winner.

When plans were floated to stall Victor's confirmation, the White House reacted with a back channel revelation that the President was not opposed to appointing his designate as an official White House advisor or even "czar" for the war pending Senate action. This would put his appointment out of the reach of the Senate. Victor was aboard Marine One with the President's party that left the South Lawn for the Presidential Maryland retreat. The Senate confirmed the President's nominee without any delay.

Officially Camp David is a military installation and not precisely located on maps of the area for security reason. It is both a rugged and comfortably appointed haven in the Catoctin Mountains about sixty-two miles north-northwest of D.C. The staff and primary security is provided by both the U.S. Navy and the Marine Corps.

The media didn't miss the fact that Mrs. Deidra McAffie was also in the group. She had been seen and identified at Walter Reed when the President was still in a coma. Surprisingly, some members of the media acceded to the White House's off the record request to downplay the fact that Deidra was the wife of Porter's former surgical partner. Mentioning that she was the widow of his former colleague in their reports. But the press corps' gossip mill was spinning at top speed with speculation.

The President convened a meeting of his top military and intelligence advisors in the Laurel Lodge conference room soon after arriving at the Frederick County, Maryland retreat. The plans for deployment, supplies and logistics had already been well under way. Through a video conference connection, N.A.T.O. staff joined in and a list of goals and dates for the required steps were forged. Surveillance from satellites and drones were increased and intelligence reports from previous missions were combined. The attacks on ISIS and Iran were combined with the invasion of Yemen.

A working lunch was served and the group continued on through the afternoon.

In the main lodge, Irene Meehan and Deidra enjoyed each other's company and getting to know each other outside the pressure and worry of their joint hospital experience. The pair had met years before at the funeral of Porter's wife, Yvonne. The new age musician and first love of Porter's life had died in a crash between the commercial flight Yvonne was on and a private pilot who was flying into the Amarillo airport --- drunk. Porter and Deidra's husband dissolved their joint surgical practice a few months after Yvonne's death. Within a year Deidra's husband had committed suicide following a scandal involving one of his nurses. For years before the tragic deaths, Porter and Deidra and their partners had been close friends since medical school.

Deidra's feelings for Porter had become evident at Walter Reed during his extended coma. Irene, who had taken on the job as First Lady at Porter's request, was already retired with her N.A.S.A. rocket scientist husband when Porter called. Porter had additionally asked Irene's husband, Mark, to become a Special Advisor to the President because of the her husband Mark's keen insight, intellect and sense of humor. Irene had become aware of Deidra's unspoken feeling for Porter during their hospital ordeal. Page, Porter's daughter, had likewise recognized that her father had been too lost in grief and then too involved in his writing as an avoidance mechanism to realize the possibility right in front of him.

"Is the whole family involved in this conspiracy?" Deidra asked taking a sip of Earl Grey tea. "I noticed Page's name on the credit card for the airline ticket."

"Sometimes these things need a little nudge," Irene said with a twinkle.

"Well nudge ahead. I do believe he's starting to get the message."

"Not to get ahead of ourselves, but are you willing to step into the job as First Lady --- you know, *if* and *when*?"

Deidra had a good, full laugh.

"Well, '*if* and *when*' Porter gets around to asking, it will take a few months to plan a wedding --- and by that time, he can't have that much time left in office. But, yes, I am aware of what goes with this relationship."

"Good for you," Irene smiled. "Let's not short change Porter. He could be quicker than we think."

"Well --- *if* and *when*."

"No, I think it's just *when*."

CHAPTER 15

"See. It's just like riding a bike," she said.

"And a lot more fun," Porter said in the dark. "You were right."

Deidra snuggled up to her lover in the king sized bed at Camp David, Maryland. In the moonlight that leaked through the gap between the curtains and the inside window casing, they had make the full connection they had attempted that night in Amarillo when the Secret Service came knocking with the news that altered both their lives. This time Porter was aware of his need to feel that surge of life and love that only two people can share at the most intimate level.

They snuggled in the depths of the night and in the afterglow of the sweetest kind. When Porter had to pull away, Deidra was of the same mind. His body temperature not just warmed them in the Camp David lodge but on this chilly early spring night, it reached a point that even passion was overcome by thermodynamics. They had to separate to keep from soaking the bed with their sweat.

Porter pulled away, reached over and opened the bedside table.

"Like I said," Deidra said, "if that's a condom, you don't need it for me --- and it's a little late to be thinking about that anyway.'"

He didn't say anything, but the small squeaking sound of an opening ring box was evidence of what he had on his mind.

"It's time for you to make an honest President out of me," Porter said.

"There's no President I'd rather legitimize," she smiled taking the ring and slipping it on her finger in the dark. She then rolled over and turned on the beside lamp.

The three carat diamond flashed in the setting of platinum between two horizontal diamonds on each side of it.

"Porter, this is absolutely beautiful."

"Can I take that as a 'yes'?"

"No. Take it as 'absolutely' and 'I thought you'd never ask.'" She threw herself into his arms for a long, soul deep kiss.

After they had separated and snuggled back down in the covers, she put her head on his shoulder but her eyes remained on the dazzling band and its sparkling diamonds.

"Who picked it out for you," she asked.

"Me, myself, and yours truly."

"How? And how'd you pay for it. I thought all your credit cards were suspended and your bank accounts in trusts."

"They might have been, but with my lack of salary, I still needed one. But somehow someone over looked my Amazon account and my royalties in Europe. And I can still use a laptop."

"How did it get through White House security?"

"It didn't. Someone at Amazon must think I'm in the closet because I had it sent to Mark."

"Your brother-in-law?"

"I wasn't about to let Irene know first."

Deidra laughed and kissed Porter again.

"Pick out your wardrobe very carefully in the morning," he said. "Leigh Janda is with us and I'll get him to take an official engagement picture sometime tomorrow."

"You think of everything."

"Not everything, but I do try to work on the plot and what scene should follow what scene."

They made love again --- with the lights on --- and Porter delighted every moment in Deidra's beauty. She loved him but at first had to force herself to ignore his scars from the attempted assassination only to decide she had to accept them just as she did all of him.

～

After the photo was taken --- to Deidra, Irene, and Cinnamon's approval, Porter had a meeting with Graham Newcomb, his Chief-Of-Staff and Grant Yarbrough while the ladies were starting to plan the fall wedding.

"The next major things I want to tackle are that full press conference I've been promising, and then I want to finish that speaking tour --- starting in Milwaukee."

"Milwaukee?" his Press Secretary asked. "Is that a good idea?"

"Grant, I don't want Milwaukee to get the same wrap Dallas got after Kennedy. Those people are not to blame. I want to go back there so they and the world will know it. In fact, let's try to get the baseball stadium if we can."

"The Brewer's stadium?"

"That's it. I don't know the name ---"

"Miller Park," Newcomb said.

"Good," Porter picked up. "Give the Secret Service and the city time to set it up. From there let's finish the rest of the tour --- all the way to California --- plus I want to add Hawaii, and Anchorage, Alaska. I want the whole country to feel like we're in this together."

"Yes, sir," Grant noted in an ever present reporter's notebook he'd been carrying since he started as a TV news reporter.

"Have things smoothed out with Congress on Victor's appointment?"

"They have," his Chief-Of-Staff said, "but ---."

"But?" Porter repeated.

"There's someone I want you to meet, Mr. President."

"Porter, Graham, we're all on this. You, too, Grant," he said to his Press Secretary.

"Yes, sir," Graham said and sighed for not using the President's first name. "Do you know a Washington lawyer named Felix Alvarez?"

THE RELUCTANT INCUMBENT

"I think I met him once --- at some Congressional function. Isn't he the one they call 'The Godfather' of politics?"

"Yeah, I've heard of him, too," young Grant said.

"That's what they call him," Newcomb went on, "but not in a mafia kind of way. He knows everybody --- and where all the bodies are buried --- but he's not into manipulating people or twisting arms. He's more of a --- compromiser --- deal maker --- in a good way. He's never been a politician himself, but he's friends, good friends, with people on both sides of the aisle."

"I've heard," the Press Secretary said, "that he can get people together who wouldn't even speak to each other in the hall or on the floor of Congress."

"That's him. He likes you, Mr. --- Porter," the Chief-Of-Staff corrected himself. "And I think he would be a good man to know --- officially and unofficially. Talk to Vice President Ives. I think he helped her at least once while you were still in the hospital."

"I'm game," Porter said. "Get me some background on him and set up a meeting. But let's do this press conference soon and then the trip."

"Sir, sir," both men said to the President in unison

CHAPTER 16

"Walk to the White House holding hands," Cinnamon advised. "It will be the media mystery of the day."

"Are you sure?" Deidra asked glancing at Porter as they flew over Washington in Marine One.

"With all the people at Camp David --- and you *know* everybody there told everybody here --- this is not going to be a secret long. We'll prepare a press release with a photo for tomorrow a few hours before your press conference. Let the press chew on it overnight. Everybody loves a mystery," Cinnamon said with a wink.

The President waved to the media with his free hand when he and Deidra exited the plane but they answered no questions.

"You see what it's going to be like?" Porter asked Deidra as they walked through the cool spring morning.

"And it's too late to change my mind?" she joked.

"Way too late," he said giving her soft hand a loving squeeze.

Felix Alvarez, a dark skinned Hispanic in an understated three piece, pin stripped black suit, spent the next few hours in the Oval Office with the President, Chief-Of-Staff Graham Newcomb, and brother-in-law Presidential Advisor, Mark Meekan. The short attorney used his diminutive size to disarm those around him with self-effacing "short jokes" until the point became mute. It was then that the subtle and dynamic personality of the consummate deal maker began to emerge.

Porter liked the man right off, as did most people, he later learned. Felix was open in his body language and his acceptance of new acquaintances.

"What I can do for you, Mr. President, if you'll allow me, is to improve your relations with Congress. You are aware that when you called them out in your State-Of-The-Union speech, you made a lot of enemies."

"I knew I would before I said my first word," Porter said.

"Well, the good news is that you also made more friends in both chambers than I think you know. There are some very good people who came to this town to do what you have been able to accomplish in a very short time. They admire you for it. But, unfortunately, many are low ranking mavericks who buck their leadership and don't get plum committee assignments. But after the fall elections, they're going to be emboldened. The handwriting is already on the wall and the old congressional guard knows it. The question is, 'What was your net value before you went to Washington and what is it now? Can you explain the difference?' And, of course, the corrupt can't and will try to avoid answering --- but the public, thanks to your call --- is going to demand accountability.

"A few will still slip through," the President said from his arm chair to Alvarez who sat on one of the couches.

"Without a doubt," but all the money they're going to have to spend on the next election cycle is worrisome — even for each party. A very narrow margin of victory, if possible, could weaken their importance when they get back here. We could be looking at a very different Congress in the future. And I will make it my goal to know all the new people and where they stand."

"Graham tells me you don't play games or twist arms."

"Not my style, Mr. President. I believe in building open and honest relationships with people and then being able to reason with them. I don't win all the time --- but I have a pretty good batting average. I know some people don't like me and never will --- and I respect that --- but as long as they will still take my calls and talk to me we can exchange ideas. When I'm wrong, I admit it --- when someone has a better idea --- I say so. I have changed my position and the position of those I work for when it's the right thing to do."

"So no smoke filled rooms with wine, women, and song?"

"I see myself as kind of a postal worker, Mr. President. I deliver the message, on time, under all circumstances and I don't tell tales or keep secrets. That's what makes what I do so different in this town. I'm in a service business --- I'd like to see everybody play and everybody win."

"It sounds like we are on the same page, Mr. Alvarez."

"That's what I thought the first time I heard you speak, Mr. President."

"But nobody does much in this town without a quid pro quo."

"True, but what I'll ask will never be anything that will compromise you. Sometimes a visit to a state for you, or a photo op, even an invitation to a White House event for them. Those are the kind of currencies I deal in --- but usually with the approval of your Communications or Press Secretary first."

"And in exchange?" Porter asked.

"Take that Ogallala Aquifer problem. I believe I can get support from some members of both houses in all eight affected states to address this."

The Ogallala Aquifer is one of the largest aquifers in the world. It's a shallow water table located beneath the Great Plains of the American West. It lies under parts of Texas, New Mexico, Oklahoma, Kansas, Colorado, Wyoming, Nebraska, and South Dakota. It takes about 6,000 years for rainwater to replenish the 174,000 mile water system. The reason Porter ran for a seat in the U.S. House from Texas was to call attention to the problem and address it in a way farmers and ranchers of the High Plains could not just live with, but support.

"The Speaker is going to be a problem there, I think," Porter said.

"Perhaps not. Vincent Sturges made you a promise when you agreed to take on the Interim Speaker's position before last Christmas."

Alvarez's understanding of the issue showed he had done his homework. Porter was impressed.

"He did but now that he's Speaker he has been very upset that our little agreement kept him from becoming President."

"Yes," Alvarez said, "but I think you'll find that Vincent Sturges is still very much a man of his word. Why don't we see if I can deliver on that before we talk again?" he suggested.

"Deal," Porter said reaching across and taking the attorney's hand.

"And while I'm at it, I think I can feel out some people about their continued support of the terrorism war."

"I'm very interested in keeping this conflict focused and it not becoming a money maker for those in the military hardware business."

"Understood, Sir."

CHAPTER 17

The lectern on the podium in the White House Press Room was replaced with an overstuffed armed chair with a small table and a glass of water. On the chair was a sign which read, "The Hot Seat."

"Ladies and gentlemen, the President of the United States," the smiling and never camera-shy Press Secretary Grant Yarbrough announced as Porter came in and everyone stood. The President crossed to the chair and picked up the sign with a chuckle and handed it to his black/Vietnamese Yarbrough who took it away with an impish grin.

"Please be seated," Porter said to the media.

"Before we begin let me say a couple of quick things. First of all, there are no questions out of bounds --- but we've all seen enough legal dramas on TV to understand the phrase from an objecting attorney, 'Asked and answered' --- meaning that the question has already been asked and answered --- the attempt by the opposing council to ask the question in another way in order to get a more favorable response has legally been already asked and answered. That's the way I will deal with any endeavor to get a 'got 'ya' way of trying to come at a topic from another direction when we've already dealt with it. Ask your questions anyway you like, but make sure you get all your nuances covered the first time. There are too many topics we should cover here today for us to rehash a few subjects over and over. As I said, nothing is out of bounds, but once we've dealt with it, let's --- I hate to use these words --- but let's 'move on.'"

The reference to the theme of President Bill Clinton's supporters and both the on-line site and then organization, MoveOn.Org, got a laugh from the media. The movement's purpose was to get the public and the press to abandon their obsession with the Oval Office oral sex scandal between then President Clinton and Monica Lewinsky and focus on other stories.

"And lastly," Porter said as the room quieted, "the only reasons I won't answer a question is either because, one, I really don't know the answer --- in which case we'll get you the answer and Grant Yarbrough will answer the question tomorrow. Secondly, I won't compromise the security of the country or any of our men and women serving in or out of uniform. I trust you'll understand that when something is *classified*, there's a reason for it.

"Beyond that's let's have at it."

There was an order to who gets to ask questions in the Press Briefing Room and in what order. The wire services were given the first crack because they serve newspapers, cable and broadcasters around the world. Next the broadcast networks and major cable news outlets had their chance. The key national newspapers and newsmagazines were followed by prominent internet news sites and, finally, regional newspapers. The protocol was that each reporter stood holding the wireless hand microphone, identified him or herself and employer before asking his or her question.

The first question: "Mr. President, are you comfortable leading the country and by extension leading us into a war since you came to the office without being elected?"

"God help anyone who is comfortable going to war," Porter said. His voice was being picked up, amplified to the room and then sent to each video camera and audio recorder in the room via Bluetooth wireless technology. "I am very aware of my status both as an unelected President but also as the legal and legitimate Chief Executive and the Commander-In-Chief of all our armed forces by our Constitution.

"Additionally I know what war really is. I've seen it, felt it, and I've had the victims of war slip away in my hands. I've lived with the fear you can only experience in a war zone 24/7/365 --- for multiple tours of duty. These last are qualifications I wish every person who holds this office would have. It informs my decisions at profound levels for which those who only know war through the movies and TV can't possibility grasp. But most importantly, as President, I have seen this great nation shrink away from its duties and responsibilities at home and abroad. Our unwillingness to step up to past affronts and challenges has greatly contributed to our being the target we are today. As of now, that is no longer who we are. Attack our citizens --- especially our children --- and there will be no place for you to hide.

"No, I am not comfortable --- but I am capable and I am resolved that this war which has been forced upon us will be concluded in such a way that others will be forewarned."

The questions about what exactly the U.S., N.A.T.O. and other willing allies would do Porter did not answer. "This," he said, "is for our military to show and not for me to tell."

Another reporter wanted to know when the "shock and awe" of this war will begin.

"I *won't* tell you that," Porter said. "But believe me when I tell you that when it starts --- you'll know. It'll be in all the papers and on every available TV, cable and Internet outlet. And I won't tell you how long it will last --- no one knows that. This is not a war with a beginning and end date. We will do the job until it's done. Period."

In response to a question to list those joining us in the fight, Porter said that information was classified for obvious reasons. But he did confirm that there were Muslim nations in the fight on our side.

About his attempted assassination he told one of the network's reporter, "You'll have to get answers about the man under arrest and the status of his prosecution from the Attorney General's Office and the F.B.I. I have chosen to step aside and insure that no personal feelings or attitudes about this event will taint the legal process in anyway. Trust me; it's not because I don't care, but I understand my position and the best thing I can do is to back off. Besides, there are other things, much more important things going on right now that should and will have my attention."

The President's proposed Constitutional amendments, Porter stated the fact that the Balanced Budget Amendment was still in the House were all congressional matters involving money began. The Senate had the Congressional Term Limits amendment. Beyond that all Porter would add was, "I made my statement and my case in the State-Of-The-Nation address. It is now in the hands of the American public."

A cable reporter asked, how his relations were with Congress?

"*Strained* would be a mild adjective, I think. I knew when I spoke up I was making waves --- and even tsunamis --- but it was something I thought needed to be said and I was in the unique place of being able and willing to say it. The recall process now is one only the American public can resolve. And no matter how it comes out, I am working on finding a way to work with Congress. That is part of the job description."

For two hours President Porter Randall took questions. He was glad to have the water handy.

His toughest questions were about his recovery and his personal life.

CHAPTER 18

"As a former surgeon, and fiction writer, how are you finding the Presidency?" one of the bloggers asked as Porter's news conference continued.

"I found it at my front door in the middle of the night in the form of Secret Service Agents," Porter said with a grin.

The laughter from the media was instant and loud.

"I'm sorry," Porter told the reporter when he stopped laughing himself and could speak. "That was just too easy to miss."

Again chuckles filled the room.

"The serious answer is this job is nothing like what anyone on the outside can imagine. The pressure never lets up. Only the big problems come here. All the smaller ones are handled by those who aren't worried about reelection --- and more of them are good, competent, compassionate people who are working to served the American public. While it's the slackers, the disreputable, and the crooks you people mostly report on --- there are hundreds of thousands of government workers who daily go about their jobs with pride, dedication, and respect from delivering your mail to helping our veterans --- most of us never hear about them. My job is to take the heat, to take the pressure, and make the difficult decisions as best I can."

"Given your attempted assassination and long coma, Mr. President," a woman from the B.B.C. asked, "do you think you are up to the task?"

"By myself --- no --- with God's help and the assistance of those closest to me --- without question."

From a different TV reporter known to be openly liberal in its reporting on everything came this question, "This morning we received the press release about your engagement to your ex-partner's wife. How long has this relationship been going on?"

"Congratulation, Mr. Moss. You succeeded in getting your 'got ya" question in. Let me ask you one. It's a journalism 101 classic, 'Do you still beat your wife?'"

The atmosphere in the whole room changed instantly.

Abner Moss was a well-known ambush style reporter who specialized in trapping people with his carefully crafted questions.

"Your question is built on a false premise and like mine to you, there's no way you can answer it without creating more problems for yourself than you address. First of all, let me correct your mischaracterizations. I am a widower. My fiancée is not the wife but the widow of my former, not ex, partner. Our relationship goes back more than twenty years when her husband, Darren McAffie, my best friend, my wife, Yvonne, and I would double date to the cheapest dinners at home we could devise to save money--- and rerun movies we'd watch on TV because we were all too busy, too exhausted, and too poor going to medical school to do anything else. Mrs. McAffie is the godmother to my daughter. In the few years since her husband's suicide and my wife's death in an airline accident, we have been friends --- nothing more or less. When I awoke from my coma and found her asleep with her head on the side of my bed in the middle of the night, one of my very first revelations was to became aware of what a kind, caring, and considerate person she had always been. I asked her to marry me this past weekend at Camp David because I love her."

Not one to be shamed for his brazen verbal attack, the reporter shot back, "Are you two sleeping together?"

"That is classified information. It comes under the heading of 'Need To Know' and you sure as hell don't. It's none of your damn business.

"Now sit down," Porter ordered the pear shaped little man, "and pass the microphone to someone a little less offensive."

The reporter complied and the next reporter looked at the microphone as if it were contaminated before she spoke.

"Mr. President," she said, "were you surprised at the speed with which the Senate approved your nomination of Victor Chesterfield as Secretary of Defense?"

"Not so much surprised as very pleased. It is good to see the whole government pulling together in these times. Let's face it --- who would turn down a Congressional Medal of Honor winner and long-time Washington power broker like Mr. Chesterfield for a position he is clearly qualified for --- and at a time when his service is truly needed?"

"Is this one of the steps you are taking to making nice with Congress?"

"To some extent. But remember, Presidents and Congress are rarely simpatico --- even when they represent the same political party. Our forefathers expected there to be conflict --- that's one of the checks and balances they built into our form of government. Likewise, the Supreme Court has its role to play. There will always be differences --- and there should be --- or a President can become a tyrant --- Congress can become a corrupt institution driven by corporate bribes and personal vendettas --- and even the Supreme Court can become so out of touch with the country that they are making laws from the bench or changing existing laws to meet the agenda of the judges. It's not a perfect system --- but like Winston Churchill said, "Democracy is the worst form of government --- except for all those other forms...."

There were a few, "asked and answered" responses from Porter in the next few minutes. It quickly became evident that the major topics had been covered and there was actually a lull when Porter sat forward.

"Thank you for coming today. I know we both get paid to be here, but this is what journalism should be all about. Please continue to do your job --- fairly and accurately --- because our way of life depends on you as much as it does on this office, Congress, and the courts. I do want to apologize for taking so long to get around to this. I plan on doing it once every two months at least from now own. That's a promise. Give me a day or two either way --- but that's the plan. And as you should already know, we have done some opening up of this --- the People's House --- to pool reporters and photographers.

"Good afternoon."

Porter rose and left the Press Room as the reporters scrambled to their feet and a few even applauded.

CHAPTER 19

In his morning briefing Porter heard headlines from all over the country, each emphasizing whatever part of the press conference that particular outlet happened to single out --- whichever fit the narrative that it wanted to report. One of the minor stories to come out of the news conference was that cable TV reporter, Abner Moss, had been fired. He had proven to be such an embarrassment that his company could not be seen standing behind him.

Overall the coverage was generally favorable. One headline read, "America Has A Leader Again." Another proclaimed, "President and Congress *Strained*." Still another took the soft approach printing, "Wedding In The White House Future." Several reported some variations of "Prez Not Comfortable With War - But Determined."

The planning for the upcoming war was on track as Porter's briefers reported. While China and Russia grumbled, the number of nations joining in the fight continued to grow. No "D" date had yet been set but the process was narrowing. The F.B.I., state, and local police had captured or killed most of the perpetrators of the school bus attacks. Terrorist cells were broken up and members were arrested. Several lone would-be terrorists were taken into custody with stockpiles of arms and explosives hidden in their apartments, homes or storage lockers. People living in the same house or next door were totally ignorant of these people and their plans.

When Porter had a few minutes to himself, he had his personal secretary, Gwendolyn Jacobs, get Dr. Alexander Estes, Head of the Texas Tech Medical Emergency Department in Amarillo on the phone. The, fit, 60 year-old, black physician was a full colonel in the Army Reserve and had been tapped by the Secret Service to be Porter's temporary Presidential Physician on the flight from Amarillo to D.C. the night Porter found out he was suddenly President. Estes and Porter knew each other from social functions in the medical community but were more colleagues than friends.

"Colonel," Porter addressed Estes when Ms. Jacobs buzzed him that the call was ready.

"Mr. President," the surprised doctor answered.

"Do you have a minute to talk?"

"I do."

"There is a packet of medical records I'd like to send you. What I'm asking is for you to look over it as a physician and tell me what you think. I don't want to prejudice your examination so I won't say anything more about it."

"Not a problem, Sir."

"And please keep this between the two of us. If you want to consult with anyone you trust, all I ask is that you stress that this is private."

"Got it," Estes said.

Porter could imagine the man running his hand over his close cut salt and pepper hair as he often did.

"Then I'll say no more. The package will be hand delivered to you. When you have some conclusions, please call me back at this number. Ask for Ms. Gwendolyn Jacobs. She will get you to me."

"Yes, Sir."

"And thank you ahead of time."

Both men hung up without any more conversation. Porter explained to Gwendolyn what was going on and asked her to get him one more number before she took two packages from him for special curriers.

When she buzzed him again, Porter was able to speak to Texas Ranger Captain Konner Ochoa. The two had met one night when Porter happened to be on duty in Amarillo's Northwest Hospital E.R. The 47 year-old Ranger came in with a bullet wound from an attempted convenience store heist. The pair had hit it off and become friends. Over the years Porter had asked Ochoa for specifics on police procedures for some of his novels, and the Ranger had also had a hand in helping Porter and Yvonne adopt their daughter, Page.

This conversation was pretty much a repeat of the previous request for a medical review from Col. Estes. The difference this time was that Porter was asking to send video. It had been the Ranger Captain who had caught the scam a woman had tried to pull on Porter earlier that year. The woman, a grifter, claimed that Porter had fathered a 'love child' by the woman while he was in Florida on a book signing tour after his last novel had come out. It was the Ranger working as a private detective for Porter who had found the evidence that proved the lie. This time, the President was asking his friend to examine video footage and see if he could see anything out of the ordinary.

Like the doctor, the lawman agreed to help with a minimum of explanation from the President. Porter gave Konner the same contact information and rang off.

After dinner Porter said his good bye to Deidra before the limo took her to her return flight. He went to bed early and was up early. The new day was the resumption of his interrupted cross country trip after his State Of The Union speech. This time the theme wasn't the point of the speech but a rallying of support for the war effort --- not that much rallying was needed. The nation was clearly behind their Commander-In-Chief but he felt it was still a good opportunity to "show the flag" --- really show himself as a recovered President who was capable of leading.

Air Force One touched down at Milwaukee's General Billy Mitchell International Airport before eight A.M. It was in a hangar of this very airport, named after a city's native son, where Porter had been shot. But the President wasn't thinking about his own history here but the man for whom the airport was named.

Mitchell grew up in Milwaukee and became a famous military aviator who today is considered to be the father of American air power. He flew early bi-planes in France during the First World War and was promoted to Brigadier General as he commanded all U.S. air efforts in that conflict. He was appointed deputy director of U.S. Air Service in the years following the war. The maverick officer forcefully pushed for increased funding of U.S. air power. When he proved that bombers could sink battleships, where most military expenditures were going in those post WWI days, he made many enemies in the military establishment.

In 1925 he was *returned* to his permanent rank of colonel from his wartime appointment as a one star general. Not content with his demotion, his enemies court-marshaled him accusing him of insubordination for accusing Army and Navy leaders of "almost treasonable administration of the national defense" for refusing to invest in aircraft carriers over traditional battleships. He resigned from the service shortly after the trial.

Like so many visionaries, Porter reflected, Mitchell's contributions weren't fully recognized until after his death. It was Franklin Roosevelt who promoted Mitchell to the permanent rank of Major General, three stars, posthumously.

To himself Porter repeated Lincoln's words, "All we can do is the best we can do."

But this time President Randall was not destined for a Mitchell Airport hangar. Instead it was across town to Miller Stadium, home of the Milwaukee Brewers, National League Baseball team. The retractable roof was open to a beautiful blue sky and a capacity crowd of forty-seven thousand plus.

There was a heartfelt welcome from the crowd for Porter which roared for over ten minutes before everyone took their seats and introductions were made by the mayor and governor. When Porter could finally speak, he said, "Now as I was saying…."

He had the crowd instantly --- and they loved it!

CHAPTER 20

The rest of the day Porter crossed the country over to Minnesota, down to Iowa, Kansas, and Oklahoma before ending the day in Ft. Worth. Then it was off to Santa Fe, Denver, Boise, down to Salt Lake City and Phoenix, L.A., and Seattle.

To his audience in Los Angeles he said, "Hollywood, as in all past conflicts we need you. I would ask you to look to the heart of America, not just in what you call 'fly over country' between here and New York, but in the soul of all Americans. Give us stories that bring us together --- stories that appeal to our better angels --- stories that will honor and empower those who will be putting their lives on the line so that you can continue to do in freedom what you do. To those who feel the calling --- and I know there are many among you who do --- earn the uniform of choice and join the ranks of those who have always made America the land of the free because it is the home of the brave."

In all the cities where there had been children killed, he met with grieving families to assure them he understood their pain. He emphasized that this war was not of our making, but one we would win. He reported how recruitment had shot up for all the services and that our volunteer services would be a force for freedom and justice.

The only reference he made to the State Of The Nation speech was to say that any law, rule, regulation, or interpretation of the law and the Constitution that was good enough for the American public, should also apply in full measure to Congress, the Supreme Court, and to the Presidency. This always drew thundering support from the crowds.

The last day he awoke as Air Force One touched down in Anchorage. Here as in all his other stops, Porter pointed out how important it was that each state retain its own identity, and unique approach to life and liberty.

"Our forefathers foresaw each individual state as a small democracy unto itself. This means the states are closer to the public than we are in D.C. Here you are closer to your officials and your laws. As the Tenth Amendment points out, 'The powers not delegated to the federal government by the Constitution, nor prohibited to the States, are reserved *to the States* respectively, and therefore *to the people*.' When we in Washington get too big for our pants and try to take over rights that are yours, you need to stand up and say so.

"For any of you who have had children in diapers, you know what it means when your kids are too big for their pants --- and Washington can be full of it, too." It was always a laugh line.

Porter was exhausted as his plane left from the last stop, Honolulu, on the island of Oahu. He had spoken at the airport and taken a respectful side trip to Pearl Harbor and the U.S.S. Arizona Memorial before beginning the long trek back to Washington.

He was surprised when his cell phone rang. It was one of the most restricted phone numbers in the world. It had to be someone on his staff he thought as he looked at the "Private" readout on the phone.

"Hello."

"Mr. President," a strange voice said in a definite Western U.S. accent. "This is Alder Mathers --- of the Oklahoma Mathers."

"Am I supposed to know you, Mr. Mathers --- and how the hell did you get this number?"

"No, Sir. We've never been introduced and don't eat off the same range. But have your people check me out. You'll find I'm all right and a good friend. As to how I got your number, well, Sir, when you've got money, there's not much you can't get --- one way or the other."

"Okay, Mr. Mathers, what can I do for you?"

"Not a thing, Mr. President. I know you've just taken off from Hawaii and you must be tired as a field mule after a very long day. I just wanted to introduce myself and let you know that there are a lot of folks you never heard of who admire what you've been through and what you're doin' for the country."

"Appreciated," Porter said a still a little suspiciously.

"You got a right to be cautious of somebody out of the blue like me callin' you on a restricted line --- but don't be. There's really no reason to get your long johns in a bunch. I've got no hidden agenda and I ain't askin' for nothin'. I'm just a nobody --- oh hell, I'm a very, very rich son-of-a-bitch --- but under it all, I'm just a plain spoken, ordinary person who happened to hit the lottery of life --- but I believe you're the best thing that's happened to this country since Harry Truman..

"What I *can do* is be someone who might be able to be of some help to you sometime, somewhere --- officially or off the books. I'm too old to join up for this fight, but I'll be behind you all the way --- helping in every way I can. Check me out and just know you've got one ol' rich Okie in your corner when push comes to ass kickin'.

"Sleep well, Mr. President, and God bless you."

The line went dead.

Porter sat in his chair at his desk looking at his phone another minute trying to process what he'd just heard when it rang again. This time it was his Chief-Of-Staff back in D.C.

"I hope I caught you before you went to bed, Mr. President."

"Graham. Good to hear from you. No bed --- but I'm on my way. Tell me do you know who Alder Mathers of Oklahoma is?"

"No, Sir. Never heard of him."

"Well, find out for me, will you?"

The news from Graham Newcomb was that the A.C.L.U. had won the first round of its suit to stop the President's move to require English only for communication with the Executive Branch.

According to Graham, the Attorney General didn't have his A team on this case. Porter told his Chief-Of-Staff to call the A.G., Winchell Hardwick, and make it clear, "I expect his best litigators on this case. If we lose for lack for effort on his part," Porter said, "let him know I am going to fire him very publicly and unequivocally. Make sure he knows he's not working for Leo Gibson anymore --- and that reality had better become evident in his performance and those in his department. Make sure he has a crystal clear understanding on this."

"Gladly, Mr. President."

Porter had one more call to make before he shut off his phone and went to bed.

CHAPTER 21

There was no doubt in her voice this time that Porter had caught Deidra in the middle of her night's rest.

"Sorry to wake you," he said.

"It's the next best thing to the real thing." She said trying to wake.

He looked at his watch. "It's just after 7 P.M. here --- Hawaii. What time is it there?"

"A little after midnight. When do you get back to Washington?"

"I haven't asked. I know it's about nine to ten hours depending on head winds."

"Then you'll need several days to recover from jet lag."

"Yes, there's that. I'm counting on Graham to keep my schedule in such a way that I can get to bed early for a couple of days."

"Oh, I'm sure he will. He'll not want you to yawning in the middle of a meeting."

"God, the press would love that," he laughed.

"I can see the headline now," Deidra said, "'President Asleep At The Switch.'"

"'Again!'"

They laughed together.

"I've got a state dinner this week. The new president of South Korea and his wife. Interested?"

"I'd love to, but there are still so many things to do here. Page is driving up day after tomorrow from Lubbock to help me with the invitation list. I talk to your sister every day. And Cinnamon connected us with Mrs. Jacobs --- what a wonder she is. Not only does she know who is who, but she knows who can sit at the same table with whom."

"She's worked years in the Pentagon and knows everybody who is anybody --- and usually their secretary who really does all the real work."

"In her case it's almost true. She's the best personal secretary I could have ever asked for. But she works so most people don't even know who she is or what's she's done."

"At times," she said, "I've wanted to throw up my hands and have us just go to Vegas and get married by some Elvis impersonator."

"I know what you mean. If you want to do less, just say the word. A White House Wedding was supposed to be a gift --- not a burden."

"Porter, it is a gift. I love the idea …."

"But the realities are more than you bargained for?"

"It will work out. I promise."

"Another thing I wanted to talk to you about is --- I'd like to come visit you --- there --- two weeks from now."

"Can you? I thought you weren't taking any more vacations."

"The truth is it's not going to be much of a vacation. It'll be a lot like Camp David. A working vacation."

"Well, I remember the nights, so it's okay with me."

"I love you," he said.

"And I love you, Porter."

"One more thing," he said a moment later. "I'd like to make your ranch my official home base in Amarillo."

"It's going to be your ranch, too," she told him.

"Well, the Secret Service will need to crawl all over the place and set up a command center."

"There are plenty of old buildings here they could use --- as long as they don't mind what it looks like from the outside."

The ranch Deidra owned had been in her family for four generations. It was both a working ranch and tourist destination for horseback riding, bike trail paths, and camping sites. All of it was based out of what was left of a real western town of Adobe Walls at the mouth of Palo Duro Canyon. The reconstructed town had been used as a set in several movies and had been restored enough to have a working saloon, general store, blacksmith forge, stone church, jail and a few arts and crafts shops in some of the old buildings.

"They will love it."

"Then tell them to come ahead. I'll get my foreman to work with them."

There were a few moments of silence between the two as she heard the deep throated roar of the jet engines from Porter's phone.

"Why did it take us so long?" he finally asked. "Why did it take my being shot to wake up?"

"Oh, Porter, we had both been through so much grief."

"But we had so many years of shared happiness with Darren and Yvonne."

"And their ghosts were always with us."

"But I know they would have wanted us to wake up and discover what was right there in front of us."

"There are none so blind," she said.

"Amen. I am so glad the 'sleepers have awaken.'"

"Have we moved from the Bible to Dune?" she laughed.

"Seems like it," he joined her chuckle. "What if we use the Dune theme in the wedding --- it would be something only we would get."

"I love it," Deidra said. "'The sleepers have awakened.'"

"This sleeper needs some rest."

"Me, too. Thanks for calling, Porter."

"Thank you for being there Deidra. I love you."

CHAPTER 22

A front page editorial of The New York Times captured the new reality for the nation's liberals. Emmett Dillington, the intellectual, spiritual, and out spoken voice of the left, wrote the column which precisely made the point others had thought but hadn't found the words to articulate.

WHAT DO YOU DO WITH A PROBLEM LIKE RANDALL
By
Emmett Dillington

I'm showing my age by referring to Roger's and Hammerstein's THE SOUND OF MUSIC from the late 50's to the mid-sixties. The film for 1965 and countless high school, college, community and professional stage productions over the years have, however, kept it alive so I'm hoping my references aren't totally archaic.

The story of the play and the movie is of a postulate, Maria, who plagues the Mother Abbess because, as good hearted as young Maria is, she's simply "not an asset to the abbey." I see the same parallel with our Accidental President, Porter Randall, and our country. You can't help but like the man, he has been wounded and spend months in a coma and I have no doubt that his motives are pure. The truth is, however, he's so wrong about so many matters that I can't help believing he's simply not an asset to our nation.

Not since the days of John F. Kennedy, have I witnessed a press so captivated by a President. In case of Kennedy we had a truly towering figure who undoubtedly put his country before himself. He, in fact, lost his life trying do right by his country. Can we say the same for Randall? I don't believe Porter Randall is a John Kennedy.

First of all, the man is in the most powerful office in the world through circumstances so extraordinary they are worthy of a Hollywood Oscar for sheer imitation. We don't live on the silver screen, in a universe of special effects and plot twists to bring the hero home in triumphant. We live in the real world. It is in this world that the actions and words of our latest media darling is leading us astray. We know what happens when the press doesn't do its job. We are watching it happen again.

Without a doubt he is "a flibbertigibbet, a will-o'-the wisp; a clown." He's made us all laugh but is that what we need as a leader? The Presidency is not a gig for a stand-up comic. It is a job for someone thoughtful, wise, experienced, cautious, and determined.

Randall has already attempted to divide us in the disguise of uniting us with a common language? We are all in debt to the A.C.L.U. for taking up the cause no single one of us could mount. They have won in the first court but undoubtedly this administration will continue the fight all the way to the Supreme Court if necessary. Does the language of Shakespeare truly need an executive order from the office of the President of the United States? Why must we all fit into one man's model of a modern American citizen? We are, always have been, and always will be, if there is any justice, a nation of immigrants. Any attempt to deprive any of us of our native tongue, customs, dress, or culture is an assault on us all.

Can the unspoken will of the people in the form of political correctness be overturned by the stroke of a pin? We agree to the common sense and social justice of political correctness without a national referendum and bring about needed changes in our language and actions through the power of social pressure. How is that not enough? Now it has all been swept away because one man doesn't like it. Is that just?

We are now in the middle of a major Constitutional amendment process because an unelected President doesn't like the legislative branch of our government functions. The very same Congress he was a part of for two terms he now has problems with. The fabric of our separate but equal branches of government is being undermined at the behest of a naïve interloper. His attempt at nobility by claiming he doesn't even need the income of a working politician is hardly what it appears.. I'm convinced that somehow Randall lives more in his world of popular fiction than in the practical world the hard working Americans must face every day. He would have us reshape our legislature to fit his vision instead of to service the public in the ways our long time political leaders have learned to do through their experience and mastery of the legislative process.

He has called for two amendments to alter how our government works. He would force Congress to balance a budget which not even the hand of God could balance with even his devotion to the military. He doesn't seem to care much about the social program that has made America what it is today. He wants Congress to be forced to cut funds to those who need our help the most. This President would shred our safety net for the elderly, the poor, and those struggling to find work when there is no work to be had.

And now he has encouraged us into a war at a time when we are at out most vulnerable. Yes, we have been attacked and yes our children were the targets. But where is the money going to come from to mount this new Army and Navy we'll need to succeed in what he's called, "World War III?" He likes to show us his religious leanings and asks for prayers. Where is his Christian forgiveness? Where is his turning the other cheek? Will we not at least try for peace before we resort to war? He says he knows war. If he does, why is he so willing for us to engage in it again and on such a scale?

Our new President is becoming a darling to some in our once critical press and the enemy to anyone who disagrees with him. Like the song in the musical, "…he's a lamb, a riddle, a child! There are so many things we'd like to tell him; so many things he ought to understand. He's a flibbertigibbet, a will-o'-the wisp, a clown."

But we're not laughing.

CHAPTER 23

It was a surprise to Porter to see his Secretary of Defense at the morning Presidential security briefing.

"Victor," the President said as he crossed to his chair and the usual group stood in front of the couches which faced each other in the Oval Office. Grace Spurlock, Porter's National Security Advisor in her normal suit accentuated by a single strand of pearls and fashionable glasses was across from the bald Metal of Honor winner. Also in attendance were brother-in-law advisor, Mark Meehan, Chief-of-Staff, Graham Newcome, Communications Director, Cinnamon Higdon, and Press Secretary, Grant Yarbrough.

"Good morning, Mr. President," the group said out of sync with each other but of the same mind.

"Good morning," Porter answered. "I see by the front page of the Gray Lady," as the New York Times was commonly called, "Emmett Dillington isn't a fan."

"He's not totally in support of anyone to the right of Marx or Lenin," said Mark Meehan. "He's even been known to call out far left fringe Democrats for being too conservative."

"If Dillington isn't unhappy with somebody or something, he isn't happy," Cinnamon said. "He seemed to be trying a little too hard ---

'he protests too much.' It will be interesting to see which networks even pick up on his remarks."

"Victor," the President again looked at his bald Secretary of Defense. "Do you need to go first?"

"It's a heads up, Mr. President. Boko Haram in Nigeria has kidnapped two-hundred and nineteen Christian school girls and has taken them to Chad, right next door."

The African Islamic terrorist group called Boka Haram advocates a version of Islam which forbids any political or social activity associated with Western society. The name "Boko Haram" in fact is often translated as "Western education is forbidden" or "Western influence is a sin" and even "Westernization is sacrilege." Included in their laundry list of forbidden pursuits are voting in elections, women wearing shirts or trousers as well as receiving a secular education, especially girls and women.

"The President of Nigeria has appealed for help." Victor Chesterfield continued.

"To us directly?"

"Yes, but also to anyone who will help."

"What are we doing?"

"A Delta Force Team is in route. They were doing training in Morocco and left at three o'clock this morning --- at my direction. They won't do anything without your approval, Mr. President."

"They've got it. Do you need it in writing?"

"No, Sir," Victor said, "Your verbal okay is good enough."

"When do we expect something?"

"Tomorrow night their time --- late afternoon our time."

"Are we close to setting a 'D' day?"

"Yes, Sir. Very close. We are moving assets around the clock."

"Excellent. Anything else I need to know?"

"No, Sir, not at the moment. You are in the loop and will be updated as we progress."

"Thank you, Victor."

"I'll be back here tomorrow afternoon," he said getting to his feet.

"See you then."

THE RELUCTANT INCUMBENT

Everything else security wise in the briefing the Secretary of Defense knew so he left the meeting and returned to the Pentagon.

As the meeting was drawing to a close, Cinnamon asked, "Are we going to respond to the U.N. Security Council emergency meeting? Ambassador Quill keeps stalling, but he either needs a statement or you need to go yourself, Mr. President."

"I am not going to go to the U.N. to beg for permission to defend ourselves."

"Shall we have Ambassador Quill say that?"

Porter thought for a moment then said, "No. I think I should be one to do it. How soon can we schedule it?"

"Any time," Cinnamon answered.

"Then let's make it late this morning. Clear the schedule and let me fly up there before noon."

"That's pushing it," Graham said. "The Secret Service likes a lot more lead time than that."

"Fair enough. They still won't like it but let's do it tomorrow, first thing. Set it up."

"Yes, Sir."

"What's on the schedule today?"

"The big thing is a meeting this morning with Clement Nance, Chair of the Republican National Committee."

"And what's the purpose of this?"

"It's a courtesy call. But being a professional politician, I'm sure he has a wish list."

"Do doubt," Porter said.

Two hours later the slight man of five feet nine inches was showed into the Oval Office. Porter shock hands with Nance and offered him a seat on the couch across from where the President sat down. Clement Nance was a frequent TV and radio talk show visitor on all the networks. He was freckled with a thick head of red toned brown hair and prominent "Betty Davis" eyes. His voice was almost raspy but not quite.

"How are you, Mr. Nance?" Porter asked.

"I'm fine," he said. "How's your wound?"

Porter felt his chest and said, "No problem."

"Unless the weather is about to change. Am I right?"

Porter nodded.

"I picked up a little shrapnel back in Iraq." He pulled up his left pant leg to show the scars of a long ago injury. "It's my onboard weather forecaster no matter what the Weather Channel says."

"Sometimes days before," the President agreed. "Now, what can I do for you?"

"I'm not here selling anything, Mr. President. Honestly."

"You don't want me to appoint more Republicans to open federal positions?"

"Well, of course. We both know that goes without saying --- and I didn't come here to say it."

"But you do have a question?"

"Right on. Simply put, we all know you're an independent but have you completely ruled out a run for this office in the next cycle? I know what you've said in your speeches, but we would be proud to support you if you have a change of heart."

"I am not on the market and I don't intend to be. While that leaves me without political allies, it also frees me to do things no one can do merely because I am politically free."

"We get that --- but things change. I just wanted to let you know that if things change to such an extent that you have a change of heart, you will find a receptive audience in the RNC."

"The offer is appreciated, Mr. Nance, but it also comes with strings --- no matter what you or anyone else says. It's the political reality of party politics. Without those strings I am much freer --- albeit severely time restrained. Remember, I didn't ask for this job. As soon as I'm out of it, the happier a lot of people will be --- including me."

CHAPTER 24

The United Nations' main headquarters building is in Manhattan and has extraterritorial rights, meaning it and its members are exempted from the jurisdiction of New York City, New York state and United States laws. This extraterritoriality extends not just to the iconic building in New York but also to the other principal U.N. offices in Geneva, Switzerland, Nairobi, Kenya and Vienna, Austria, to those nations, cities, and states.

The Security Council, the real power of the U.N., meets only in New York in its own high ceilinged, open and well-appointed chambers. It has fifteen members at all times. The winning powers from World War II, the U.S., the U.K., France, Russia, and China are the permanent and only veto powered members of the council. The other ten non-permanent members are elected by regions for two year terms. Only Israel has been barred from membership on the Security Council because it is believed that the U.S. will always look out for the interests of the Jewish state. No Muslim nation has been so barred.

When President Porter Randall took the U.S. seat at the huge semi-circular table, the U.S. U.N. Ambassador, Walsh Quill, the distinguished dark skinned, black man with angular features, full mustache and a wide, gap toothed mouth, sat in one of four deep baby blue chairs positioned behind each nation's place at the table. Fifty year old Secretary of State, Dr. Clara Sonnenberg, occupied another chair with her curly, dark blond hair swept back over one ear. Presidential Advisor Mark Meehan was in the last chair.

This month's rotating Security Council Chair, the U.N. Ambassador from Denmark recognized Porter as soon as the session began.

"Ladies and gentlemen," Porter said looking around the table at the delegates. "I am a man of plain words and clear meanings. As I told some members of my staff yesterday, I will not come to the U.N. to seek approval or to ask permission to protect our national sovereignty.

"We have been attacked in an intentional, brutal, and savage manner by agents both domestic and foreign whose aim it is to terrorize the United States and our way of life. They have long pledged to bring their twisted and evil ideology to our shores and subsequently to the whole world. They have, since these cowardly attacks on us, brazenly proclaimed responsibility for the senseless murder of children on their way to school. It is one of their stated goals to die a martyr's death in the service of their cruel and blood thirsty deity. Let there be no mistake in the minds of anyone at this table or around the world --- it is *our* goal to arrange for as many meetings between these fanatics and their cruel god as possible.

"We do not want your permission or your blessing or even your tacit approval either by your looking away or your neutrality. We welcome any nation who feels as we do that there are evils in this world which must be confronted and annihilated. This corruption of religion in the name of ignorance and male superiority cannot be condoned.

"The first goal of a nation/state is to defend its population and those in its recognized territory, air space, --- as well as its natural resources both within its territorial and its extraterritorial sea lanes, oceans, rivers, and lake borders --- and the right to exist in peace with others in this world on the same terms.

"Sun Tzu thought of war as a necessary *evil* --- but one which must be avoided whenever possible. So it is with The United States.

"Still, when it is time for war, the first goal of war is to defeat aggressors --- be their advances by land, sea, air, space, or cyber intrusion --- through saboteurs, acts of terrorism, unfair trade practices, currency manipulation, corporate espionage and intellectual/creative property rights.

"The United States of America has neither territorial nor sovereignty ambitions nor do we seek to dominate, rule, or coerce any individual or population to live in anyway but in peace. As human beings, our time on this earth is relatively short. We see no reason it should be under duress from governments --- foreign or domestic.

"And yet, it must be understood that the United States will stand by its N.A.T.O., S.E.A.T.O. and other treaty obligations to friends and allies. We will not be harassed, tortured, or forced because others wish it so. We offer peace, honor, justice, and fairness and expect the same from others.

"Aggressive nation/states and political/religious organizations attempting the violent overthrow of other nation/states are the enemy now and forever.

"Nation/states which do not, nor will not, live in peace with their own people or with their neighbors and other nation/states --- nor act in good faith according to agreements and/or treaties --- forfeit their right to exist. Tyrants, despots, and controlling regimes are among these.

"So, my message to you is simply this; join us or get the hell out of the way! We are doing this and no power on this earth is going to stop us!"

There was some applause both from other members of the Security Council and from some people seated in the red chairs of the gallery.

Porter waited a moment before he concluded.

"One last word --- and this is to all members of the United Nations. This organization has long failed in its missions. The best successes have been in creating, maintaining and growing a corrupt bureaucracy. Even its humanitarian efforts have been distorted and misguided because its first aims have gone to the awarding of bribe riddled contracts and black market/under the table deals. If this does not change --- and change quickly, the United States will no longer have any interest in participating in this high minded, low achieving, dishonest organization. The U.N. was started with the best of intentions, but it has long abandoned any serious efforts to live up to its own ideals.

"Clean this house --- put it in order --- or we will simply go our own way."

The rest of the U.S. delegation got to its feet with the President and walked out.

CHAPTER 25

Outside the U.N. chamber walking with his Secret Service escort through the halls toward his waiting car, the President turned to the U.N. Ambassador.

"Ambassador Quill, we've not had much of a chance to talk. I appreciate your silence during my address. But you came to this job with much different expectations, I'm sure. I am not and never will be in the mold of President Gibson. If you'd like to terminate your tenure here, I will understand."

"The thing is," Mr. President, "I was very surprised to get this appointment from Leo --- we were fraternity brothers in college. He was a poly sci major and I was in business. I made my pile in some very lucky stocks early on. And I've continued to do well at it. Leo and I played golf over the years and I liked the man. When he began to make a name for himself in politics, I contributed to his campaigns over the years. I've never been into politics and didn't much care for one party over the other."

Their heels sounded on the marble floors as the group progressed through the building.

"Once I got here," the Ambassador went on, "I came to understand what really goes on behind the scenes --- and, as you said, under the table. I was ready to call it quits here last Christmas --- and then Leo died. When you came to office, I discovered I did care about what went on in politics more than I ever thought I would. I agree with everything you said back there.

"I think I can do this job," the U.N. Ambassador went on, "with a clear conscience and more than a little back bone. I'd like to become a real pain in the ass to some of these blowhards. I would be proud to continue to serve if you'll have me."

"Done," Porter said shaking hands with the Ambassador.

The text of what became known as The Randall Doctrine, Porter's words to the Security Council, was flashed around the world. It was both a challenge and a warning.

On the continent of Africa as darkness began to fall, camouflaged soldiers were readying to drop from stealthy aircraft on a mission of mercy.

Two hours after dark a single blacked out combat cargo plane passed an open grassland, and four parachuted Green Berets leaped into the night in two pairs. Sixteen minutes later the same craft returned and settled onto the grass guided by infrared lights planted at the secured boarders of the make shift runway by the first four soldiers. The craft came to a near halt before reversing directions for takeoff. However, instead of hurdling back into the air, its back doors opened and its cargo was discharged. Twelve silent, electric powered dirt bikes zipped off the into the dark. Each was guided by the night vision goggles mounted to the helmets of the drivers, semi-automatic rifles slung over each soldier's back.

Four miles away the target of the raid was the camp of circled Land Rovers, pick-ups, Jeeps, motor cycles, and open transport trucks. This was the Boko Haram guerrilla band which had their prize, the two-hundred-nineteen Christian girls, huddled together in the center of the temporary base. Several thousand feet overhead, a unmanned drone which had picked up the group hours before and tracked them to their present location, now pinpointed their location. That information along with the infrared representation of every human body and heated motor was being relayed via satellite to Delta Force, H.Q. at Pope Field and Fort Bragg, North Carolina, the Pentagon, the situation Room in the White House, and the heads-up-display on the face plates of each soldier of the mission.

The small group of the 1st Special Forces Operational Detachment-Delta, (Delta Force) hurried carefully through the high grass for a few minutes until their leader, a figure who looked like all the rest, stopped, dismounted and set the kickstand on his silent electric dirt-bike. Every soldier unslung his or her rifle, checked the silencer on the end of the barrel and repeated the process with their specially designed holstered .9 mm pistols. The leader cupped his hand to his mask covered throat and said, "One." In turn all the others counted off and adjusted their headsets clipped to an ear. The leader gave a hand signal and the team fanned out to prearranged positions around the darkened camp.

From the Situation Room the President could only watch with the Vice President, Secretary of Defense, the Chairman of the Joint Chiefs, Porter's intelligence security briefing team and his most trusted advisors --- Chief-of-Staff Newcome, Presidential Advisor Meehan, Communication's Director, Cinnamon Higdon, Press Secretary, Grant Yarbrough and White House Photographer, Leigh Janda. Also in attendance were Speaker of the House, Vincent Sturges, and Senate Majority leader, George Tossen, both of whom were bewildered to be summoned to the White House in mid-afternoon. The whole assemblage sat in the dimly lit room watching the large video screen with the overall infrared picture of the scene from the drone as well as the multi images split on a single screen --- this last the collection of the night vision cameras of each Delta Force team member.

A half hour or so later the drone images showed the Special Forces soldiers take up their positions and hold in place. A command,

"Ready," was spoken by the leader. At once all the soldiers began to move toward the camp.

At the whispered command, "Hold," all the soldiers froze in place. One of the soldier's image moved back away from his or her position. The moving image showed that this soldier was slipping into a ditch. A moment later the hushed female voice said, "Body language of the captives. One girl in the center is shaking and crying. All the others are leaned away from her. She may be wearing a bomb vest."

There was another pause in the action before the voice of the commander was heard saying, "Possible remote trigger. Seven and eight. Take out the leader first."

The female soldier moved back to her previous position. Two soldiers approached the single tent. From their night vision cameras the back of the tent was slit open by a razor sharp blade and two soldiers entered the dark tent.

The leader of the guerrilla band was clearly snoring on a cot. A remote control switch was taped to an outstretched open hand. A pair of wires ran up his arm to a cell phone in a chest pocket. One soldier positioned himself near the out stretched arm and the other stood over the sleeping bearded man. The camera on this second soldier nodded three times. On the third nod the soldier beside the open hand grabbed it and the man's thumb. At the same instant the other soldier shoved his combat knife up under the leader's chin and into his brain. He jerked only slightly and was dead.

The same knife that had killed the leader now cut the tape securing the double wires from the remote switch to the cell phone. The phone was extracted from the pocket where it rested. The wire into the headphone jack of the cell phone was yanked out and the command, "Go" was given over the headsets to all the other Delta team members. It was hard to know who gave this command but it was easy to assume it was one of the two who had removed the remote threat and the leader.

Within four seconds all the Boka Haram, terrorists, awake and on guard or asleep, were dead of a silenced bullet in the head --- except for one who slept with an open map on his lap. This one was jabbed in the neck with a needle and instantly unconscious.

The camp was searched for other soldiers. But every infrared image from the drone figure was accounted for.

In a clear voice, the mission commander on the ground said, "Stage one complete. Initiate Stage two."

CHAPTER 26

Over the next twenty minutes the screens in the Situation Room of the White House were a blur of activity.

On the ground, the Delta Force soldiers rechecked to insure all the terrorists, except for their one captive, were dead. They then moved into the cluster of girls, and one of the team members spoke to them in Nigerian. The girl in the center was separated and her suicide bomb vest was removed. As soon as she was freed, the mass of other girls enveloped her in hugs and supports which were evident even from the drone's infrared camera over a mile above. Everyone in the Situation Room was relieved and warmed by the silent display.

Four Boeing long, twin rotor, CH-47F Chinook heavy lift helicopters swooped in and landed within twenty-five yards of the camp. The cigar shaped machines with props mounted on either end of the crafts, opened and the kidnapped girls were divided into groups and hustled aboard the choppers. Within six minutes all the planes were again airborne and gathering speed to over one-hundred-seventy-five miles per hour as they flashed through the night at a little over one hundred and fifty feet off the ground.

The Delta Force team had rigged all the vehicles using the explosives of the bomb vest plus a pound of C-4 they had brought themselves for this part of the mission. Soon they were back at their rendezvous point where they had parked their dirt bikes. Using the Boka commander's cell phone remote, the explosives were set off and all the vehicles were left to rot and rust in place.

When the team arrived back at their own awaiting transport plane, they ran their bikes up the ramp, parked and secured all their arms and gear. The craft was buttoned up and with all back on board, the engines cranked up and the plane roared down the grass runway and took to the air.

Less than a half hour after the helicopters had left the kidnap camp, they radioed a distress call to a secured airfield in the town of Maiduguri in north-eastern Nigeria, the capital of the state of Borneo. The four Chinooks set down at the far end of the one runway and each discharged their load of girls into the waiting arms of a prearranged Christian community. When the last girl was on the tarmac, the war planes beat their way into the air again and raced at almost two hundred miles per hour to the Gulf of Guinea in the Atlantic. A squadron of F-35 Lightning fighters waited for them and flew escort for the choppers and the Green Beret filled transport.

The signal "Saratoga" was beamed from the transport and repeated twice before all radio traffic went silent.

In the White House there were cheers.

"Mr. Secretary," the President said to Victor Chesterfield, "and General Evans," he said to the four star Chair of the Joint Chiefs. "this was a superb night's work. I want to personally award a Presidential Unit Citation to Delta Force."

"We will arrange it, Mr. President," the General said.

"Victor," the President turned once more to his Secretary of Defense, "you know how this works. All questions about this operation will be directed to your shop. The responsibility for the mission is mine, but you handle the publicity. You know what you want to give away and what you want to keep secret. It will be totally in your hands."

"Thank you, Mr. President," Victor said.

"I do suggest, however, that we allow Nigeria to say something about this first and we only respond after others have made our actions public."

"Agreed.

"Ladies and gentlemen," Porter said to the room, "I give you the best military in the world." He gestured to the now dark video screens as the room broke open into cheers and applause.

As the group was filing out, General Evans caught up with the President.

"Sir," he said, "I think you should know that there was a little bit of collateral damage."

Surprised, Porter stopped and turned to the hawk nosed, blue eyes general.

"Tell me," the President said concerned.

"It was a lion."

"Lion?"

"A female. She was out hunting when our first people parachuted in. She thought one of our guys would make a nice meal. She attacked him while he was gathering up his chute right after he landed. She just didn't count on his Beretta. Three nine mil slugs later, one of our men had a trophy. While the team was out releasing the girls, the guys at the plane brought the dead cat back. They plan to have her stuffed and mounted in their company day room."

Porter roared with laughter.

"General, that's a great story. Let's make sure it get's told."

"Even if we didn't have a hunting license in Chad?"

"Look at it this way, Boka Haram didn't have a kidnapping license."

"No, sir, they didn't."

"And our people weren't hunting --- they were just protecting themselves."

"How about the prisoner we captured?"

"He's trussed up like a pig going to market," Victor said joining the General and the President. "There's a lot he's going to tell us before he ever sees daylight again --- like where they get their funding --- who plans their missions?"

"All within the Geneva Convention, I trust," Porter said.

"Of course, Mr. President," the Secretary of Defense said in such a way that Porter couldn't tell if he should believe his bald administrator or not.

CHAPTER 27

Over the next twenty minutes the screens in the Situation Room of the White House were a blur of activity.

On the ground, the Delta Force soldiers rechecked to insure all the terrorists, except for their one captive, were dead. They then moved into the cluster of girls, and one of the team members spoke to them in Nigerian. The girl in the center was separated and her suicide bomb vest was removed. As soon as she was freed, the mass of other girls enveloped her in hugs and supports which were evident even from the drone's infrared camera over a mile above. Everyone in the Situation Room was relieved and warmed by the silent display.

Four Boeing long, twin rotor, CH-47F Chinook heavy lift helicopters swooped in and landed within twenty-five yards of the camp. The cigar shaped machines with props mounted on either end of the crafts, opened and the kidnapped girls were divided into groups and hustled aboard the choppers. Within six minutes all the planes were again airborne and gathering speed to over one-hundred-seventy-five miles per hour as they flashed through the night at a little over one hundred and fifty feet off the ground.

The Delta Force team had rigged all the vehicles using the explosives of the bomb vest plus a pound of C-4 they had brought themselves for this part of the mission. Soon they were back at their rendezvous point where they had parked their dirt bikes. Using the Boka commander's cell phone remote, the explosives were set off and all the vehicles were left to rot and rust in place.

When the team arrived back at their own awaiting transport plane, they ran their bikes up the ramp, parked and secured all their arms and gear. The craft was buttoned up and with all back on board, the engines cranked up and the plane roared down the grass runway and took to the air.

Less than a half hour after the helicopters had left the kidnap camp, they radioed a distress call to a secured airfield in the town of Maiduguri in north-eastern Nigeria, the capital of the state of Borneo. The four Chinooks set down at the far end of the one runway and each discharged their load of girls into the waiting arms of a prearranged Christian community. When the last girl was on the tarmac, the war planes beat their way into the air again and raced at almost two hundred miles per hour to the Gulf of Guinea in the Atlantic. A squadron of F-35 Lightning fighters waited for them and flew escort for the choppers and the Green Beret filled transport.

The signal "Saratoga" was beamed from the transport and repeated twice before all radio traffic went silent.

In the White House there were cheers.

"Mr. Secretary," the President said to Victor Chesterfield, "and General Evans," he said to the four star Chair of the Joint Chiefs. "this was a superb night's work. I want to personally award a Presidential Unit Citation to Delta Force."

"We will arrange it, Mr. President," the General said.

"Victor," the President turned once more to his Secretary of Defense, "you know how this works. All questions about this operation will be directed to your shop. The responsibility for the mission is mine, but you handle the publicity. You know what you want to give away and what you want to keep secret. It will be totally in your hands."

"Thank you, Mr. President," Victor said.

"I do suggest, however, that we allow Nigeria to say something about this first and we only respond after others have made our actions public."

"Agreed."

"Ladies and gentlemen," Porter said to the room, "I give you the best military in the world." He gestured to the now dark video screens as the room broke open into cheers and applause.

As the group was filing out, General Evans caught up with the President.

"Sir," he said, "I think you should know that there was a little bit of collateral damage."

Surprised, Porter stopped and turned to the hawk nosed, blue eyes general.

"Tell me," the President said concerned.

"It was a lion."

"Lion?"

"A female. She was out hunting when our first people parachuted in. She thought one of our guys would make a nice meal. She attacked him while he was gathering up his chute right after he landed. She just didn't count on his Beretta. Three nine mil slugs later, one of our men had a trophy. While the team was out releasing the girls, the guys at the plane brought the dead cat back. They plan to have her stuffed and mounted in their company day room."

Porter roared with laughter.

"General, that's a great story. Let's make sure it get's told."

"Even if we didn't have a hunting license in Chad?"

"Look at it this way, Boka Haram didn't have a kidnapping license."

"No, sir, they didn't."

"And our people weren't hunting --- the were just protecting themselves."

"How about the prisoner we captured?"

"He's trussed up like a pig going to market," Victor said joining the General and the President. "There's a lot he's going to tell us before he ever sees daylight again --- like where they get their funding --- who plans their missions?"

"All within the Geneva Convention, I trust," Porter said.

"Of course, Mr. President," the Secretary of Defense said in such a way that Porter couldn't tell if he should believe his bald administrator or not.

CHAPTER 28

Sunday Porter went to church again at the New York Avenue Presbyterian Church in D.C. and on Tuesday he went to Ft. Bragg in Fayetteville, N.C. There he presented the Presidential Unit Citation to the 1st Special Forces Operational Detachment --- Delta Force. He also awarded each team member of the Boka Haram mission a Bronze Star with "V device" for valor.

Speaking to the unit he said, "You look so much different in the light of day. The last time I saw you, you were all little light green blips on video screen or green distorted night vision faces from body cameras. I've got to say, either way, you look pretty damn intimidating."

The soldiers of the unit took that as a supreme compliment. They cheered.

"Thank you for your service; thank you for your bravery; thank you for your duty and your honor. You make us all proud. God bless you and the nation you service."

At their dismissal command, the sky turned green with berets tossed in mass from every man and woman there, and the shouting and cheering was captured by the media.

THE RELUCTANT INCUMBENT

∼

No sooner had Dr. Leonard Millhuff reached his office at Water Reed from the North Carolina trip in the President's entourage than he was whisked back to 1600 Pennsylvania Avenue, arriving by limo. As Presidential Physician, Dr. Millhuff, had chosen to continue to practice his healing arts at the famed hospital rather than hang around the Executive Mansion bored out of his mind but always at the President's summon.

The Chief Usher, Mr. Jewell Weilding, greeted him and ushered the guest to the hallway outside the Oval Office.

"Would you mind leaving your medical bag and your cell phone here?" short haired Secret Service Agent Melissa McBride asked standing at the door to the oval office.

"Of course, not," he said surrendering both before Presidential Secretary Gwendolyn Jacobs opened the door and announced the visitor.

Millhuff had been in the Oval office before; so he was not daunted by the room or it's trapping of power. He had been expecting this meeting to receive some kind of Presidential plaque, metal or reward for his efforts on Air Force One when he saved the President's life. What wasn't expected was the video screen set up in front of the marble fireplace, F.B.I. Director, broad shouldered, white blonde haired, Leon Nickleby, and two other "men in black" standing behind the couch be was directed to.

President Randall brought over a thick folder and laid it down on the coffee table before he sat in his usual arm chair and the 60 year old Nickleby took a seat on the couch opposite Millhuff.

The doctor didn't say a word but tried to take in what was going on around him.

The grey/green piercing eyes of the F.B.I. Director seemed to cut right through Millhuff before the President spoke.

"Dr. Millhuff, we have a couple of things to show you and then a question," the F.B.I. leader said.

Ah, so it was a medical problem. "Of course, Mr. President," the doctor said.

Nickleby opened the folder and spread out the obvious medical records across the table.

"There is no rational reason I should have been in a coma for over two months," Porter began. "No one --- being in general good health ---- should have, either."

Suddenly there were droplets of sweat in the physician's hair across his forehead.

"We were all mystified, Mr. President," Millhuff said.

"And it puzzled every expert who has seen these records."

"Exactly," Millhuff summoned his poker face and his best bedside voice as he put on his glasses and pretended to look at the print out before him.

"Even more of an enigma is this," the F.B.I. Director said picking up a remote control and bringing Porter's Walter Reed hospital room up on the screen.

Dr. Millhuff enters the room when family members are dozing, and he steps over to the bed and leans over the barely moving body of the President. As the doctor starts to leave the frame after his examination, the Director freezes the image.

"I checked on the President regularly."

"Do we need to play these games?" Nickleby said. "You know we've figured it out and so do you. There's a syringe in your right coat pocket and you just injected the President in the left arm pit with its contents. You did a good job of concealing your actions --- misdirection with your left hand while you pulled up the President's arm and injected him as the camera is blocked. All those years working your way through medical school as a magician came in handy."

Millhuff was now in almost flop sweats. He could no longer hold it together and slumped back into the couch.

"The only things we don't know," Nickleby went on, "is what was in the syringe --- and more importantly for whom you did this?"

"When you leave here," Porter said after it had all sunk in on Millhuff, "you'll either be under arrest for treason and facing a death sentence --- or --- you'll be wearing a medal as a part of your disguise because you will be working for your country once more --- this time as a double agent."

It all spilled out then. The names of the Watergate Group which confirmed what Victor Chesterfield had already told the F.B.I. Director. Then the name of the drug and the name of Yale Gallagher came spilling out. Gallagher was a multibillionaire, international banker, generational moneyed Irish revolutionary, far left Socialist extremist, and currency manipulator. He was the money and the power behind the Watergate Group Victor Chesterfield never knew.

When a composed Dr. Millhuff left the White House, he was wearing a Presidential medal pinned to his breast pocket and carried the printed, framed, and signed proclamation for his efforts in behalf of the President and the U.S.

Agent McBride joined the President and the F.B.I. director in the Oval Office after Millhuff departed.

"His phone is bugged, so is his medical bag, his car, his office, home, the apartment of his mistress, and his three hidden burner phones --- one in his office, one in his car, and one at home."

"There's also a bug in the medal you gave him, Mr. President," Nickleby said, "plus one in the frame of his citation. If he burps or farts, we'll know when, how much, and what caused it."

CHAPTER 29

One of the legends of the American West centers on two battles that took place at a spot in the Texas Panhandle called Adobe Walls. The site today is part of The Adobe Walls Ranch which Deidra McAffie owns at the mouth of Palo Duro Canyon along Texas Ranch Road 217. It's outside the boundaries of the State Park named for the canyon and has sights and trails used and seen through the eyes of Americans plains Indians, early Spanish explorers, buffalo hunters and western pioneers.

The restored adobe town was built from the local dirt and grass and backs up against one of the side canyon walls. In 1864, the ruins of what had been a fort there were the site of one of the biggest clashes on the Great Plains. Kit Carson, an Army scout and colonel, fought the First Battle of Adobe Walls with 335 soldiers and 72 combined Ute and Jicarilla Apache scouts. They opposed more than one thousand Comanche, Kiowa, and Plains Apache. In the end Carson lead a retreat of his forces before they could be surrounded and massacred. The newspapers of the day painted Carson as a hero, but he always saw it as a lucky escape for the men he led. History knows it as the First Battle of Adobe Walls.

THE RELUCTANT INCUMBENT

The Second Battle of Adobe Walls, was ten years later; June 27, 1874. This time the combatants were 700 Comanche warriors and twenty-eight buffalo hunters and town's people including only one woman. The settlement was a known trading post and stopping off point north of the Canadian River in the largely unmapped sea of grass known as the Llano Estacado, or the Staked Plains, where the Spanish drove poles into the ground as a way to help them find their way.

By the mid 1870's, the few remaining free-ranging Southern Plains Indian bands --- Comanche, Cheyenne, Kiowa, and Arapaho --- saw the revitalized settlement and the buffalo hunters it helped as a significant menace to their way of life and even their existence.

Among those taking part in the Second Battle of Adobe Walls was a Comanche Chief who became famous over the years --- Quanah Parker, the child of a captured white woman, Cynthia Ann Parker.

On the side of the town's people and the buffalo hunters was a 20-year old adventurer/gambler/reporter and lawman, Bat Masterson and Billy Dixon, later a Medal of Honor winner for his actions in a different Indian fight. The fighters suffered four fatalities and the Indians about 15 the first day, a total of 30 braves by the end.

On the third day of the siege, late in the afternoon, the buffalo hunters, using their high caliber, long range, Henry repeating rifles and Sharps heavy duty firearms, were keeping the attackers at a distance. That was when Billy Dixon took aim with a "Big Fifty" Sharps --- .2 ½ inch shell, .50-90 --- at the Comanche chief who was leading the attack. In a shot calculated later to be 1,538 feet or about nine-tenths of a mile, the slug caught the warrior full in the chest and killed him instantly, throwing his body from his horse.

This shot was such a shock to the Indians that they recovered their chief's body and abandoned the fight.

The historical impact of the Adobe Walls battles were that they led to what became known as the Red River War (1874 – 75). This war resulted in the ultimate confining of the Southern Plains Indians to the Indian Territory, what is today Oklahoma.

Porter knew the history of the Walls and had visited the ranch many times while he and his wife Yvonne were raising their daughter Page, and they shared the friendship of Deidra and her husband, Darren who was Porter's partner in their day surgery practice. This time when a weary looking President slowly made the walk from the White House to Marine One, he stopped long enough to answer a question about his taking time off.

"It's not a vacation," he said. "There will be no golf or tennis. Dr. Millhuff tells me I do need to do some swimming. Several members of the White House staff are coming with me so there will definitely be more work than fun."

"Are you going to have time for your fiancée?" one reporter called?

"*Amorous In Amarillo?*' Is that the headline you're shooting for?" the President asked with as much a smile as he could muster.

While the reporters laughed, Porter turned and waved as he made his way to his ride.

Air Force One landed in Rick Husband International Airport in Amarillo a little over four hours later. His limo took him down I-40 West to I-27 South. They took the Ranch Road 217 exit and pulled up to the ranch house in twenty minutes.

The working headquarters of the ranch was a mile away from the tourist, historian, and photographer's destination of the restored old Western site. In fact, the main house was only partly exposed --- over half of the two stories and basement of the house were built into the side of the canyon. Great, great grandfather Russ had build inside of a wide but deep cave which succeeding generations had found as useful as did the ranch's founders. The year round temperature of the main house was seventy-two.

The Secret Service had not set up in one of the buildings in the town but in what looked like a little used tractor shed. Within a week it has been decked out, insulated, fortified, wired and hooked up to the White House and major government agencies the President might need to contact. The multi vehicle corrugated structure was walled off and also served as a site for press briefings.

Porter was greeted on the wide front porch by a blue jeans and boots wearing Deidra who took him in his arms for a big hug as soon as they were together. Once inside they went to the living room and sat awaiting the news Porter knew was coming.

At 6 PM, Texas time, the first reports came in that the first strikes of the war had been made in the middle of the night, Mid East time.

CHAPTER 30

The first few days of the war were surprising in their swiftness, destruction and relative low loss of life. It was also surprising how wide spread the attacks were. They reached from across North Africa, from Yeomen, Egypt up through Gaza, Lebanon, Syria, Iraq, Iran, to Indonesia. The very first targets were radar sites, many of which and gone dark intermittently since the U.S. and N.A.T.O. declarations of war. Satellites and drones had long marked all harden sights and were also tracking mobile sites.

AWAC airborne targeting and radar planes pinpointed sights which painted the locations and stealth bombers pummeled them. Ocean based cruise missiles screamed through the sky and took out installations which gave the rag tag enemy any eyes and ears beyond the fortresses where they hid. Stealthy drones accompanied target drones whose mission was to draw the fire of the enemy below. Once fired upon or pinged by a quickly activated radar position, the munitions of both the stealth and the traditional drones used the ground fire or signals as aiming points for Hellfire missiles and other powerful but very selective ordinance.

Injured drones would self-destruct before they could fall into the hands of the enemy.

From all this, more and more details emerged and were plotted onto command targeting screens for ocean going, airborne, and land based coordinating units. By the time the fourth generation M-1 Abrams battle tanks, the M-2 Bradley and Buffalo M-ATV Armored Fighting vehicles, the Marine LCAC hovercrafts, Humvees, armored personnel carriers, AH-64D Apache and AH-47 Chinook helicopters, got troops into the fight, the enemy was largely deaf and blind as far as technology was concerned.

In a statement to the media from what was being called the Adobe Walls White House, Porter said, "This war we did not want has begun. To the Islamic extremists I say, we do not want your land --- we do not want your culture. All we want is to live in peace. You do not.

"Freedom is way of life we choose. We allow others to choose for themselves --- even you --- if you can do so in peace. We do not want to force anyone to adopt our democratic ways. We know there are many cultures who do not want freedom --- they want to be told what to do by others. If your people want that --- it's fine with us. But do not try to force your way of life on us. It is the leaders of your culture who want war. Those are the ones we will now hunt down and kill.

"If you want to live in the 4th century and not the 21st --- do so --- but do so in peace. Until you are ready to do that, we will give you the war you want."

Before the extended weekend was over, bunker bombs had exposed hidden Iranian nuclear sites in the desert at a place known as Fordow. The mushroom cloud marked the point of the 1.2 mega ton explosion where Iran had pledged no atomic enrichment beyond twenty percent existed and swore to the world it had no atomic weapons ambitions.

Porter kept checking with Deidra as the war news kept coming in and the demands from the media mounted with every report from the front and an embedded reporters.

"This is what's it going to be like," he told her. "Are you sure you want to put up with it?"

"This kind of thing, no --- but I'm going there to be with you," she said hugging one of his arms.

He kissed her.

"I need you," he said. "Here and there."

"And I need you."

"Want to come back to D.C. with me now?"

"I wish I could. Men don't have any idea what it takes to plan a wedding."

"I'll tell you a secret. We really don't want to know."

"It's not a secret."

They shared a laugh.

Cinnamon summoned Porter back to the phone. He spent the rest of the day talking with N.A.T.O. leaders from Deidra's living room. The President's last official conversation of the day was with Victor Chesterfield in the Pentagon.

"Is it going as well as TV is reporting?"

"So, far. But you know, the first days are the easy days."

"How about the nuke in Iran?"

"It took three bunker busters to get to it. We knew it was there. I was beginning to think they'd moved it."

"And we're monitoring the fall-out so our people are out of harm's way?"

"Yes, Sir. We know where the wind is going for the next few days. Of course, the media will jump on the fact that we're getting it when it comes around the world."

"No matter how you say it, if Iran never had the nukes they claimed they didn't, there would never have been an explosion."

"It's still going to be a hard sell."

"Granted. And I'm not looking forward to that --- but it goes with the job."

CHAPTER 31

"You wanted to know who Alder Mathers was," Graham Newcome said to the President when they were alone in the President's office on Air Force One on the return trip to DC.

"I'd begun to wonder if that had fallen through the cracks."

"No, Sir, but it's easier to find out who a member of the Mafia is or even an undercover Chinese agent."

"Now, you have my attention," Porter said leaning back in his chair as the plane flew East.

Pock marked Newcome opened a zipped notebook and extracted a file. He didn't read from it as much as he used it for reference as he filled in the details.

"To begin with he's richer than God. If he were a Russian, we'd call him an oligarch. Forbes lists him in their top five hundred richest men in the world, but they don't know the half of it. He'd put Bill Gates and Warren Buffet to shame if he wanted to --- which he doesn't. He started out in oil with a small patch of land and now --- well, now, he owns or controls corporations that own or control other corporations through several layers.

"He's into casinos --- on tribal land --- plus electronics, aerospace, retail, shipping, automotives, software, computer gaming, racing, commodities, stocks and bonds --- you name it and he has money in it --- and is getting a fantastic returns from it. Most of the people who work for him don't even know who he is. But the way he runs his businesses --- the people he hires, the managers and directors he puts in charge make whatever business they're in the best of the best. People want to work for his companies --- and those who do don't tend to leave --- unless they go to start their own business with some new idea they developed while working for Mathers --- and he often finances these start-ups --- demanding only that they are good to their people and that they're not afraid to fail. If they fail, and some do, he hires them back at their original companies --- for good or until they come up with something else new and innovative.

"He's Choctaw by birth, but he was a Navy Seal --- his father and grandfather were both Code Talkers in World War I and II, each in his own time. He also owns a couple of charities that annually manage to rank among the most altruistic in the world. The thing is he does most of his charity work anonymously. He has first class hospitals in seven states and somehow the bills to the poorer patients seem to get lost somewhere in the mail."

"And what's the bad news?" Porter asked trying to absorb all this information.

"We're drawing a blank there. Nobody, not the F.B.I., not the C.I.A. or N.S.A. or anybody else can find anything to say against him. He seems to be a straight arrow --- no ethnic slur intended."

"I'll bet it's not a slur --- even in Choctaw."

"And he wants to be of help?"

"That's what he said when he called."

"How?"

"He didn't say."

"And there's nothing he wants from us?"

"From what you tell me, Graham, he could buy and sell the whole Executive Branch and never miss the change."

"True. Do you want me to set up a meeting?"

Porter thought for a moment before he said, "I do. And I'd like for it to be like the meeting with Victor."

"The Trowbridge House?"

The President nodded. He reached for a blue legal pad from a desk drawer.

"Can you see that I'm not disturbed until we get to Washington. I need to write something down."

"Yes, Sir."

When the President was alone, he began to scribble on the pad.

It took almost a week to get the meeting with Alder Mathers. When the President met the man, he encountered a muscular man of average height. He was fifty-three according to Graham Newcome's report. He had dark hair and eyes and the deep voice Porter remembered from the phone call.

"Mr. President," Mathers said as they shook hands.

"Mr. Mathers. It is a pleasure. You're a very secretive man."

"I like to think of it as 'private.' I don't owe anyone but my wife an accounting of who I am or what I do."

"If you hadn't reached out to me, I don't know I would ever have known you existed."

"If you weren't the President, and the kind of President you are, you wouldn't have. None before you have."

"Let me make sure I understand ," Porter began.

Mathers cut him off, "Mr. President, it's not complicated. I like very much who you are and what you've done for the country so far --- and I'd like to help if there is something I can do."

"Are you offering money, time, your expertise, contacts --- what?"

"Nothing --- or any and all of the above. A man in your position could likely use someone in my position --- and I'm offering to be that person."

Porter studies Mathers a moment then slowly nodded his head.

"Okay, there is something --- something I'd like done --- but something that I would like not to have either my or the country's finger prints on --- even at a distance."

"Very much within my wheelhouse. You name it."

Porter took another moment before he said, "I'd like to have a movie made."

This surprised Mathers.

"Now that's something I've never done. I do know some people --- not in Hollywood --- in the U.K. --- but they know what they're doing."

"Even better." Porter handed Mathers the folder the President had brought with him. As the multi-billionaire looked through the pages, Porter explained. "It's a story outline --- a scenario for what I'm looking for."

"Let me show this to the people I'm thinking of. If they think it's worth doing ---."

"If they don't agree that the story is good, then I wouldn't want to proceed with this."

"Good."

"But there is a time limit on this. I'd like to have this ready to premiere at the Cannes Film Festival at the end of next May or the Venice Fest in Sept."

"That's not much time."

"I know, but it's important that this get out quickly."

"I'll see what I can do, Mr. President."

"At any rate, I appreciate your offer of help," Porter said as the two men shook hands.

CHAPTER 32

Youssef and Selma
(A Synopsis)

Youssef is your typical English seventeen-year-old --- except he's Iraqi/British. Selma is a pretty fifteen-year-old French school girl --- except she's Syrian/French. They've never met and don't know each other and yet they are more alike than they are different. Both are the children of parents who fled oppressive regimes in their native countries and came to the West for a better life for themselves and their children. Youssef's father teaches physics at a small university while Selma's father and mother are both physicians.

They enjoy the pursuits of Western teenagers --- music, the latest fads, and the opposite sex. Both are popular within their circle of bright, funny, happy-go-lucky mixed ethnic friends. They have not abandoned their Muslim faith, but neither are they as fanatical about it as some people they see in the streets and on TV. The one thing they both unknowingly share is a growing interest in the on-line propaganda and chat rooms of Islamic jihadists.

Little by little they begin spending more and more time on-line absorbing the message that they had a duty to join in the fight for a worldwide caliphate. They see the images of fighters with AK-47s and shoulder mounted RPGs, the black flag of ISIS fluttering in the breeze to stirring music, while shrouded women in black proudly labor to support their warriors. The ghostly figure of martyred souls float to heaven to the chorus of hymns playing beneath the voices of challenging men and women pleading them to come and do something important with their lives --- come join the fight of the ages.

Unknown to each other, both Youssef and Selma make their plans, collect money and plan trips from their suburban homes to the Middle East. They make good their escapes and travel both by train and air, even by bus, to the hot, dusty world of Islamic jihad. They never meet and although pictures of them appear on TV monitors in the places through which they travel, they are not recognized. They both make a clean escape and chronicle their journeys on social media. They eventually arrive in crowded cities where, using their cell phones, they connect with children who take them by the hand, and lead them to men and women who take them on the last leg of their journey.

Youssef wears khaki's and tennis shoes as he lets his thin mustache and beard grow into the scraggly, unkempt sign of rebellion. When they reach their final destination, Youssef is told to strip and is given baggy pants, a home spun shirt and long vest, sandals, plus a wrap for his head. He has to be shown how to wear the wrap. His phone and I-pad are taken away from him. He is then sent to a fighter's training camp.

Selma has her attractive headscarf ripped off of her and she is slapped for being brazen. She meets a woman we get to know as Fatima, who is in charge of women recruits and the disciplinarian of the faithful women. Selma, too is stripped and is quickly shrouded in black from head to foot. She is put to work doing kitchen work of a type that is totally foreign to her.

As Youssef finishes his training and begins to soldier with the rag tag group of undisciplined fighters, he takes little regard for their own cleanliness but, like the others, he is devout in their five times a day praying. He has been changed. Fighters are taught to be are cruel and beat, wound and kill anyone of any age or sex they consider an enemy. They learn to sleep on the ground, in the backs of trucks, in the hills and eat whatever is available. They rape and then murder woman, especially Christian women, but also Muslin women who are not Sunni. This is a much uglier world than the one Youssef thought he was becoming a part of. He watches those close to him being killed or wounded and left on the battle field where they drop.

But Youssef is smart and not only picks up the language, but even learns to read it. He becomes a valuable fighter and even a leader because he is wise enough not to take stupid chances --- and because of that, other men, even older men, begin to follow his lead whenever they are around him.

Selma is deprived of her electronics, too. She has to learn to live in a world with little running water and electricity. She is often whipped and beaten because she doesn't respond to commands in the language she is still trying to learn. Life for widows and for the unmarried is a constant struggle --- leading often to the death of children and to women who volunteer to be suicide bombers.

She decides if given the chance, to be a bride to a fighter, she will take it believing that life can't get much worse --- and that was really the reason she came to this world in the first place. She remembers the carefree days in France before she left her old life --- but that is all behind her now. She is auctioned off and is claimed by a warrior. They are wed and on their wedding night, her husband, who is drunk, ugly, and filthy, rapes her viciously and she is left crying and distraught.

After a few more times with her husband, who is never pleased with her sexually, Selma is taken by a group of other women and given a clitoridectomie with no anesthesia. This is a horrible, painful scene. In the end she collapses into unconsciousness.

Youssef, now a young man with a full beard, leads his fighters into a village which is virtually defenseless as the local defense force soldiers flee when his unit arrives. He watches as his men pillage, rape and murder their way through the village. A commander arrives after the slaughter and is pleased with what Youssef has accomplished. He is promoted on the spot.

Because of his English, Youssef is given the honor of being the master of ceremonies for the group beheading of a dozen captured soldiers. He says his scripted words but does not look behind him as the kneeling men are murdered.

On another mission Youssef manages to separate himself from his men as they are being beaten back without his leadership. He hides in the rubble until an American Blackwater Operative comes by. To this man Youssef gives himself up.

Selma also manages to escape when she is supposed to be shopping one day when a rocket hits a nearby building. She boards a train and gets helped by a frightened European woman. The woman is thankful she was able to help Selma get to a European embassy in a big city.

Youssef and Selma become media sensations as they tell their stories to the international press. They are glad to be reunited with technology and given new cell phones which they have problems using because phones have changed so much --- but they both manage to get in touch with family and friends as they are being driven to yet another TV interview. As they text away in the back seat of a nice sedan, motorcycles with a driver and a gunman move up on both sides and fill the car with machine gun fire. This also kills the driver and the car flips on the highway and the motorcycles take off in opposite directions. The car bursts into flames and one of their cell phones slides away from the carnage only to be crushed by a passing truck.

In another mid-eastern another town a pair of Arabic looking but western dressed teenagers look up from their phones in the middle of the passing crowd. They see each other a moment, but then both look down as a child steps up and takes their hands and leads them away. The cycle begins again.

CHAPTER 33

Nothing takes over the news in Washington like a scandal. Around the world self-important and self-righteous politicians who get caught with their hands in the till always grab the public's ire and interest. Even more curiosity blossoms when politicians are discovered with their hands or other body parts mingled with those of the opposite or even the same sex who isn't the politician's spouse. Sex scandals seem to be more significant in the U.S. than in other parts of the world. Regardless of the nature of the scandal, it is magnified by implications of cover-ups and the complications of other crimes.

When the story of the missing female intern to Supreme Court Chief Justice, David G. Fish started, the affair between the two quickly became one of the key points of the story. The long married former Federal Judge from Georgia, a noted conservative before his appointment and often speaker on the moral responsibilities of citizenship, had all the needed elements for a major D.C. scandal.

The legitimate and tabloid media quickly reconstructed the illicit relationship between the handsome and distinguished Chief Justice and the eye-catching, dark skinned black former Harvard Law Review editor. Footage of the out-of-the-way small Maryland hotel where much of the affair supposedly took place was continually recycled along with a single still of the Justice with the intern in the background admiringly looking at her boss.

One of the speculations was that somehow the Gibson administration had become aware of the Justice's secret and had used it as leverage to gain the Chief's swing vote on critical matters before the court. It happened when Ms. Bostyn Dodge had been a court intern, and the relationship had continued for several months. The affair now had been over two years. A pattern of affairs with attractive interns was uncovered by the press with Ms. Dodge being only one of several over the years. The Justice's pattern of serial infidelity was traced back to the early years on the bench back in Georgia.

The resignation of Chief Justice Fish came without any intervention from the White House which kept its distance from the court and the scandal. The pictures of Fish's shattered wife were moving to even the most callous of reporters and political observers of Washington. The dismembered body of the former intern was discovered in a shallow grave by Indiana highway maintenance workers. The scene was in a wooded patch along Interstate 69 near Fort Wayne, her home. The focal point of the investigation shifted from the former Chief Justice to a suspected serial killer working the Midwest Interstates.

In the White House the interest from the beginning had become the appointment of a replacement for the disgraced Chief Justice.

"Who are we looking for?" Porter's Chief-of-Staff asked one morning.

"Someone with common sense over everything else," Porter told his team. "I don't care about party or anything political --- if someone knows right from wrong and can call it when he or she sees it, that's more important than ideology."

"Anything else?"

"Independent. I'd like to see someone on the highest court who isn't influenced by current fads, political correctness ..."

"Which you have outlawed," Cinnamon reminded Porter of his first Executive Order.

"For all the good it's done," Porter said. "We still have protests and calls for the most stupid 'correct words.'"

"But most judges have to be political animals or they'd never get elected to their first posts."

"Understood, but what do they do after that? I wouldn't mind someone who stood their ground and got voted out even though they were right on the facts and the law."

"That would be a hard sell," Graham said.

"Hasn't everything been?" Cinnamon smiled.

"That's the job," Porter reminded them. "And let's make sure we find someone who can be better vetted than Justice Fish was. Either somebody dropped the ball on his background investigation or they knew the truth and figured they had something they could use one day to control him."

"This sounds like an espionage novel," Cinnamon said. "Moves and counter moves. Motivations and manipulation. We're playing legal chess --- and we have to be three or four moves ahead of everyone else."

"Mr. President," Graham said, "do you ever feel like you're plotting one of your mystery novels?"

"I heard about a journalism professor in Arizona or New Mexico who was also a crime fiction writer. Someone once asked him how he could work with students demanding they adhere to the facts and then he would come in early everyday so he could have time to make up stories? His answer was that fiction was the only way he could make things come out right. In the real world they rarely ever did. I understand that. Could be that's why I like to write medical fiction. I certainly couldn't always control the outcome in the operating room as hard as I would try."

"What are the chances of our being able to control how this turns out?" Cinnamon asked.

"None," Porter answered. "It's like everything else we do --- "

They all repeated with him, "All we can do is the best we can do."

As Graham was leaving, Porter asked him, "Please have Mrs. Jacobs see if she can get Justice Isabel Greycore on the horn."

"Will do," Graham asked without asking why.

While the administration began their search for a justice, the F.B.I. and ISP, the Indiana State Police, arrested an interstate truck driver. He would stop to help stranded motorists and if it happened to be an attractive woman by herself, he would rape and murder her. Otherwise he would help a motorist or a family in need. He had been doing this for over fourteen years across the country only killing a time or two each year. When he found a suitable victim, he took it as a gift and a sign he was supposed to act.

Soon the media completely forgot about the former Chief Justice. His place in history was now solidified as a philanderer and a man whose passions overruled his sense of justice and his better nature. It was a typical D.C. story --- scandal leads to disgrace, downfall, and, as Shakespeare said of Julius Caesar, "The evil that men do lives after them, the good is often interred with their bones."

CHAPTER 34

The phone call to Associate Justice Isabel Greycore, the member of the Supreme Court who had sworn Porter in during his first televised address to the American public, was to seek her advice. The President's question was if she thought it would be okay for him to speak to what remained of the Court on a conference call about a non-case related matter? The 70 year old Justice considered the request a moment and asked if Porter was positive the conversation he asked for was not either to influence any matters currently before the court nor ones that it might face in the future? He assured her this was absolutely not about any such topic without telling her what it was he wanted to discuss with the court.

Two hours later Porter was on a conference call with the assembled justices who were gathered in Conference Room 500, the room of the Neoclassical building where the justices gather to discuss cases before the court. There were ten armed, high backed, rolling swivel chairs in the room --- one at each end and four each on both the long sides of the blue/grey topped rectangle table. That's one chair each for the possible nine associate justices and one chief justice.

The Judiciary Act of 1801 set the membership at five although the number could be as large as ten in total. The number changed over the first three quarters of the 1800s, but following the election of President Ulysses S. Grant, the Judiciary Act of 1869 set the Court's membership at nine which is where it has remained ever since. An odd number of members had been the rule to ensure a tie breaking vote in close cases.

Interestingly there was no Supreme Court building until the only President who ever served on the court successfully convinced Congress that the judicial branch needed its own space, independent of both the legislative and executive arms of the government. Chief Justice and former President William Howard Taft accomplished this in 1929 but never lived to see the completion of the project. The powerful looking finished structure was constructed largely of marble from Vermont, Georgia, Alabama, Spain and Italy.

When President Porter Randall spoke to the assembled Associate Justices, it was thru a speaker phone in the center of the court's conference table.

"Thank you for agreeing to speak with me this way," the President began. "I know how suspicious this request seems, but you'll see that it is nothing to do with anything before the court nor could it affect your deliberation over any question in the future.

"As I'm sure you must know, I have begun a search to fill the now vacant seat on the court. What I've always found strange is the bringing in of an outsider to sit in the chair of the Chief Justice whenever it becomes vacant. I see eight of the most qualified people for the position already on the court. What I want to do is to select the new Chief Justice from among you --- and another Associate Justice for a vacancy."

This was a fully unexpected suggestion to the members of the court. Porter imagined the Justices looking from one to another as the line remained silent for a few moments.

"As I read the duties of the Chief Justice," Porter went on as the court members listened, "he or she casts the first vote but has no more power or influence than those of the other members; chooses to write the Court's majority opinion or assigns it; serves as the judge in any impeachment trial of the President --- I hope I don't have to see that --- presides over any impeachment trial of the Vice President *if* the Vice President is serving as Acting President; swears in the President at official inaugurations --- although this is only a traditional role and not an official one --- serves as Chancellor of the Smithsonian Institution, and sits on the boards of the National Gallery of Art; writes the official annual report to Congress about the state of the federal court system; and serves as the head of the Judicial Conference of the United States, the chief administrative body of the U.S. federal courts. Oh, and there's a few thousand dollars more in salary than all the other Justices get. Do I have that right?"

"Yes, Mr President," one of the Justices said but didn't identify himself.

"So, I was thinking, why don't you eight decide --- if you can --- and if you want to --- who the new Chief Justice should be."

"Wouldn't that involve a renomination process?" Porter recognized the voice of Justice Isabel Greycore.

"Oh, to cross the *t*'s and dot the *i*'s I'm sure it might. But it shouldn't be a big deal since all of you have already been through that. And I would not expect any of you to have to resign your current position to move into this new one. So, if it became contentious with Congress --- and we all know things could --- then you could simply bow out --- no harm, no foul."

Once more there was silence on the court's end of the line.

"Why don't you think it over?" Porter suggested. "If, for any reason whatsoever, you feel this wouldn't be proper, I don't have to do it. But when I was in the service, I had new commanders come in who didn't know their butt from an officer's billet about the job they were suddenly thrust into --- yours truly could easily be sited as an example of that in my current position. I've also known some very capable people already on site, in place, who could do the job --- but the military in its sometimes questionable logic wants to go by the book when it doesn't have to. It seems to me that if one of you took over the Chief Justice slot, the transition would be a lot easier on everyone --- including whoever the new guy turns out to be.

"Kick this around and let me know. If there's a tie vote, then we'll just do it the regular way. Okay?"

There was more silence before Justice Greycore spoke one more.

"This is an intriguing idea, Mr. President, but I think we should take a few days to consider it."

"Not a problem," Porter said. "Give me a call when you come to a decision --- one way or the other."

CHAPTER 35

Half black and half Vietnamese Grant Yarbrough finished reading his prepared statement for the 2 PM White House Press Briefing and looked up ready for questions. What he was prepared for was questions about battle damage on the latest sorties, or the house to house fighting in the latest ISIS or Boko Haram fights or the status of the conflict in Somalia. Instead, the media had questions about totally different subjects.

The Associated Press reporter asked, "Is it true that President Randall has ordered M.R.E.'s as lunch for everyone on his White House Staff?"

"No," Grant said wondering how this information got out. "The President has asked the kitchen staff to please send him a M.R.E., Meals Ready to Eat, for himself each day. He thinks it's not too much to ask for him, as Commander-In-Chief, to be eating once a day, what our men and women on the front lines are eating."

"And he hasn't asked anyone else in the White House or the Pentagon to do the same?"

"No. In fact, it had been going on for a couple of days before I was even aware of it."

"Has he asked that the press be kept in the dark about this?"

"Not in the least. This is not a photo op or some grand gesture the President is conducting. This is something he is doing on his own."

"Can we get some video?"

"Well ---, "Grant seemed flustered but shrugged his shoulders, "I'm sure the President won't mind. But that's not the point. He is not, I repeat, 'not' trying to make a big deal out of this."

"What does he do if he's having a lunch time meeting?"

"He asked that his meal be served to him on a plate so as not to call attention to it while any guests are still able to enjoy some of the best from the White House kitchen."

"How does he like it?"

"He's had no complaints. Broccoli casserole still isn't his favorite but then it never was."

"Next question," Grant tried to get the focus of the room back on more serious topics.

From the rear of the room, standing against the back wall behind the row of video cameras on tripods, 36 year old Therese Herzog, the President's primary speech writer, admired the way Grant handled himself. She knew she had a crush on him and that he hardly knew she existed. The round glasses did little to flatter the pale, grey eyed, curly chestnut haired woman whose best feature was her intellect and her genuine smile.

"Is the President," the Fox reporter asked without referring to his notes, "going to ask the Senate to confirm his appointment of Associate Justice Brandon Zackery as Chief Justice?"

"That is correct."

"But isn't that unprecedented? Aren't all justices to the court appointed for life?"

"Right on both counts."

"Why is the President doing this? Wouldn't he be better served by appointing someone different as Chief Justice?"

"Each Justice, Associate or Chief, has a single vote. And President Randall realizes more than any of his predecessors that what you don't know about where your place is in the government, and what your job is, can do more damage than good. So why not put someone in the Chief Justice slot who has been around the Supreme Court and already knows the ins and outs?"

"Then the President will nominate someone else to replace Associate Zackery as an Associate Justice."

"Yes."

One of the other reporters in the room picked up the line of thinking.

"A President has traditionally put his mark on the Court by the selections made to fill vacancies. President Randall has no interest in doing that?"

"The concept that seems to be so difficult to grasp," Grant said, "is that this President, while not being a big government guy, doesn't think that part of his job description is to control everything he can. He has the power to make appointments to the Court, but isn't it better for everyone involved if the court works at its most efficient?"

"Is the President looking for a rock hard conservative, a middle of the road kind of judge, or someone more liberal?"

"History shows that the voting record of Supreme Court Justices before they join the court don't always align with positions they take once on this particular bench."

"Because they have skeletons in their closet which, when found, can be used to --- let's not say *'blackmail'* but at least, 'control' a member of the court?

"Yes, let's not say that," Grant joked and the reporters laughed.

"So what kind of person is the President looking for?"

"Someone with that most lacking attribute in this town," Grant said very seriously.

"An empty closet?" someone called out.

"Maybe a blue suit in it with a big red "S" on the chest?"

"How about a green lantern?"

Grant let this joke play itself out before he said, "No --- common sense. Something that's even missing from this room at the moment, I think."

This got a laugh but also some nods of approval.

"Where does the President hope to find this person?"

"When we find him --- or her --- we'll be sure to let you know."

Other scattered topics were touched on and as the briefing was about to break up, Grant got serious again.

"Tomorrow morning, the President, the Secretary of Defense, the Chairman of the Joint Chiefs and some others are going to Dover Air Force Base in Delaware."

The press knew this place and what was there. They settled down very quickly. The Air Base there is the home for the largest military mortuary for the Department of Defense. U.S. military causalities killed overseas are customarily brought to Dover before being turned over to the survivor's family. Three days earlier two IEDs had killed six soldiers in a convoy in Iran.

"We will take an enlarged press pool because I know you want to be there to show your respect, too."

CHAPTER 36

The Boeing C-17 Globemaster III sat in the open hangar with its rear cargo door open. This is the same type of air carrier that transports the President's limo so his vehicle was ready for him at any destination around the world. This day, this particular plane had just touched down from Rammstein Air Base Germany with its precious cargo of six flag draped caskets.

There was no need for the services of the Charles C. Carson Center of Mortuary Affairs because the remains had been positively identified at Landstuhl Regional Medical Center, Germany. Instead the craft was met by a squad of seven white gloved, black beret wearing, camo uniformed soldiers from the 3rd U.S. Infantry Regiment --- The Old Guard --- the oldest active duty regiment in the U.S. Army.

It is The Old Guard which provides the twenty-four hour sentinels for the Tomb of the Unknowns, the Continental Color Guard, responsible for the presentation of the nation's colors at special events across the Capitol Region, the Presidential Salute Battery, which renders honors to senior dignitaries --- at arrival, wreath ceremonies, and reviews --- plus providing the man power and formally dressed guards for full honors funerals. On call around the clock, The Old

Guard is also tasked with receiving the remains of American's fallen here at Dover, A.F.B.

The squad smartly and professionally lifts each casket from the floor of the cargo bay of the C-17 and in step carries the remains down the ramp with three soldiers on each side of the coffin and one trailing. They bring their burden past the waiting President and the other dignitaries, turn sharply and deliver the metal boxes to the awaiting hearses where family members of each of the fallen stand waiting.

The President placed his hand over his heart as did Vice President, Sundee Ives, Victor Chesterfield, The Secretary of Defense, the Chairman-of-the-Joint-Chiefs, General Evans and three other officers. What surprised everyone is that the President slowly dropped to one knee as the first remains passed. The others did not follow because of military protocol, any honor shown by the highest ranking officer was thought to be recognized as coming from everyone under his command at the ceremony.

The President had already spoken to each family one by one before the airplane arrived. It was a moving time for everyone present. When the last body was delivered to its hearse and the door closed, the President stood up and stepped over to a group of microphones set up to one side with The Old Guard, the families, and the hearses behind him.

"Everyone whoever puts on a military uniform and goes to war knows that this kind of homecoming is a real possibility --- but still the bravest and the best of us still step forward to do what no one wants to do --- but which must be done. As you go about your lives today --- going or coming from work, going to the grocery store, watching a movie, down loading and listening to music, checking your e-mail, or having a meal with family or friends --- remember --- you can only do this freely because of men and women like these. Men and women whose family now must suffer the price their loved ones paid --- for you --- for me --- for our freedom. Freedom is never free ---," the President looked back at the families and the black vehicles lined up behind him, "someone pays for it. Please pray for these families, the souls of these fallen --- and pray for the United States of America."

On the flight back to Washington the President got the news that the U.S. Court of Appeals had thrown out the A.C.L.U. case for lack of merit. According to the opinion, the President was well within his power as Chief Executive to make whatever alteration he felt was needed by the policies and practices of the agencies of the Executive Branch. His 'English Only' Executive Order did not include the nation as a whole nor either the legislative or judicial arms of the government. The A.C.L.U. announced it would appeal to the Supreme Court.

Talking in his office on Air Force One, Porter heard good news from both his Secretary of Defense and the Chair-of-the-Joint-Chiefs.

"As we expected," General Evans said, "the opposition doesn't have the training, structure, supplies or the guts for much of a fight. We're rolling over them anywhere they try to make a stand"

"Which isn't much," Victor said. "But like in all gruella wars, they want to fade back into the population and disappear. We're trying to make that as difficult as possible. We're also getting some excellent intel from the C.I.A. and N.S.A. They have some new tools to track their propaganda back to where it came from."

"And those places seem to suddenly go 'boom,'" General Evans said with a smile.

"The F.B.I., the Brit's MI-6, Mossad, and the other N.A.T.O. countries intel services are helping us root out the lone wolves."

"This sound very good, gentlemen. Are we sure we're not missing something?"

It was Victor who spoke next.

"We know we can't find and stop every nut out there. ISIS and their ilk are relying more and more on the mentally ill and even children for their suicide attacks. That's the hardest thing to stop. Not just here, but everywhere."

"How are we doing getting the main stream Muslims to step forward?"

"The Muslim kids who were killed in the bus attack here and in the Chunnel attack in England have done the radicals more harm than they ever calculated. They're used to intimidating uneducated, frightened farmers and peasants. We're now getting some voices speaking up in the media who are saying, 'Enough!'"

"It's about damn time," Porter said. "I hate going to events like we did today. We've already paid a higher price for Muslim freedom than they've ever even considered paying for us. Our blood --- their craziness."

"The sad thing, Mr. President," General Evans said, "is how willing so many of them are to destroy themselves and even the whole world to achieve their lie."

"And the bad news ---"the Secretary of Defense said, "is there is a growing amount of what we call 'chatter' on the dark part of the web we're still having trouble penetrating."

"What does that mean?" Porter asked.

"Nothing good. We may not figure it out until after the fact."

CHAPTER 37

The July 4th weekend became the biggest ever recorded "Days Of The Lone Wolf," as the BBC dubbed it. Fifty-six separate attacks or attempted attacks happened in the lower 48 states, Hawaii and Alaska were spared for some unknown reason. Without exception all the targets were "soft --- gun free zones." Shopping malls, sporting events, movie theatres, and outdoor concerts accounted for the largest causalities, but random cars on city streets and highways, plus family picnics and bar-b-cues in public parks, at lakes came in second. The death toll for the four day period was six-hundred-and-twenty with three times that many wounded. It became second only to the September 11, 2001 attack on the World Trade Center in New York City and the Las Vegas mass shooting.

On and off duty police officers as well as active duty, reserve, and military vets and armed citizens prevented or interrupted many attacks in their early stages. Like the school bus attacks months before, these assaults were coordinated but never involved more than a pair of terrorists. That most of the attackers were bearded young males was immediately apparent as photos of gunmen began to flash on the video screens, large and small. Subsequent days would reveal many a social media farewell manifesto even from a few who never advanced their plots beyond arming themselves and locating targets. The horror of their intended deed was simply too much for some would-be terrorists.

When other new sources began referring to the days of revulsion as "The Days of The Losers," psychologists and sociologists honed in on the "teen angst" angle as the underlying vulnerability of the attackers.

When President Porter addressed the nation from the Oval Office one night after the last attack, he said, in part, "It is the 'disaffected youth' --- 'rebels without a cause' who have slipped through the gaps of our openness to turn on freedom, justice and a way of life which has often given them way more they have ever earned. Freedom is a burden --- a responsibility --- an honor --- but one the weak cannot shoulder. These youngsters are getting their meaning and direction through the propaganda and highly produced videos of Muslim terrorists organizations.

"Because our education system has not been strong enough to properly teach them the true values of democracy --- because our colleges and universities wallow in self-flagellation and choose to celebrate our failures rather than our hard won successes, they dishonor those who have given them the very right to do so --- we now find ourselves the victims of our own freedom and openness. Between school and the life of an adult --- with a job, a family and a way to contribute to this world --- this is the place where the susceptible dwell.

"They are frustrated, disappointed, upset, malcontent, alienated, disloyal, dissident, hostile, antagonistic, on edge, resentful of authority of any kind, and on top of it all, they are ashamed and directionless. They are the dropouts, drug users, the hooligans, and the abandoned street people. They are all the things that rock n' roll was originally all about --- until now it has turned into a form to celebrate rage. It no longer has a longing for something unknown --- but it is a perverted vision of the value of women, of the police, society, and most of all, themselves. It rejoices in destruction and violence.

"This is the music that appeals to those trying to find out who they are and how to become the selves they want --- but they're not sure who or what that is. They want their own style of everything --- to be unique, respected --- but they don't know how to get there. This is where faith, religion, home, family and community used to come in. As we have slipped away from our own values, we have made it easy for Muslim extremists to let these young people imagine a feeling of need and of purpose --- they have given them a cause --- a mission --- something to fight for --- something to kill and destroy for.

"And this is where we as a nation --- and the West as an ideology --- have failed. In our openness --- or willingness to allow everyone --- even the cruel, the vile, and the twisted --- to have an equal voice --- we have become our own enemy --- because we do not call out those who violate what we used to know as 'truth, justice and the American way.' Given the choice, the young, the unprepared, the very impressionable --- without other demands --- the unbending, alternatives, the weak of mind, the moral-less, the committed losers --- allow themselves to become fodder to the warped ideology of those who only fane the concern and affection the purposeless seek.

"We must be careful and not destroy what generations have built for us. We have to thread a pathway between the iron fist of government censorship and control and healthy self-guided morals, justice and not revenge --- between forgiveness, openness, tolerance and self-destructive heartlessness that leads to depravity and ultimate destruction.

"As citizens, we must arm ourselves --- defend ourselves --- but not over react and become the victims of our individual rights and power. The danger of gun free zones is now clearly self-evident --- but can we allow ourselves to become the true victims of terror to the point of becoming the hostages to the fear the terrorists hope to impose on us?

"We admire those who used their strength, their arms and their legal weapons to stop those who would victimize others. Peace can only come to us through strength. But strength can also free the bully to become what even he hates the most. We can help ourselves if we use our wisdom, our morals, our best judgement, and our humility to act as our armed forces do, with bravery and honor.

"There are those among us who knew something was going wrong with these lone wolves. Those who knew but said nothing must shoulder part of the blame. It is for all of us to be aware, to take notice of things and people around us. It is not those who have nothing but hate for our way of life that will help us now. It is our police, our military, and individuals who are prepared we seek out in these times. We do not turn to those who loot, burn, and destroy.

"If you would do something to help, now is the time to step forward and be a part of the solution.

"Give your love and your support to those who are tonight in almost unimaginable pain through no fault of their own. Stand beside your neighbor with love and tolerance. Seek honest and fair justice for those who stab us in the heart. For us it is what democracy and freedom are all about.

"Please pray for each other --- for the United States of America --- and please pray for me. Good night."

CHAPTER 38

At his morning security briefing the next day there was a sense that everyone in the room was somehow responsible for what had happened. There had not been two coordinated attacks on American soil in one year and all on President Porter Randall's watch.

"Let's get something out in the open," Porter said after the basics of the assaults had been covered. "Did anyone --- any agency --- any of you --- do less than the best you could to prevent this kind of thing from happening?"

There was a shock on all faces as they looked from one to the other and the expressions evolved into resolve.

It was the natural leadership of the Secretary of Defense which propelled Victor Chesterfield to speak first.

"No, Sir!" he said with full confidence.

The President took a moment to make eye contact with every one of his National Security Team before he spoke.

"I believe you. I knew the answer to that question before I asked --- but I wasn't sure you did. Yes, I'm aware the media will now be howling for someone's head, but I don't want anyone to fall on their sword. The buck stops with me. If anyone wants more blood, let them come after mine. Remember, they can't hurt me by not reelecting me. They can impeach me if they can find an angle --- but they can't eat me. And I expect I'd be a pretty hard ol' bird to chew if they tried."

The tension eased in the room.

"Now that we've gotten that out of the way," Porter said, "let's examine the problem and see what we can do about it."

It was the D.N.I., Director of National Intelligence, Clancy Darren, "the grand ol' spy," who spoke up in his high pitched voice.

"We had a tool --- 'The Program' it was called --- which the courts and Congress all but gutted," the weathered old man said.

"As I understand the way it was being run," Porter said, "they did the right thing. Americans don't want to be spied on by their government."

"It is exactly that kind of thinking that allowed these terrorists to plan and plot right under our noses. I'll bet if we were to go back for a reauthorization of The Program, we'd get it now."

"Likely," the President said, "but the problems come when everyone in this room is gone and we have another master charlatan --- I don't think I need to name any names here --- or into any of yours --- and their agenda is, if not our destruction, but at least our humiliation or just simple 'I've earned the right to take what is yours for me and my kind' --- this would be the thing that could ultimately eat us alive from within. No, as attractive as that kind of power appears and as appealing as it is at this moment, we need to find a better way."

The clarity on the wrinkled face of Clancy Darren made itself known.

"Mr. President. One would-be terrorist is being very cooperative. We're not letting this out. The story we're going with is that he has sworn to take what he knows to his grave. We might have to arrange his death in prison before we can get him to a place where he feels totally safe. He's a mixed up kid who thought he bought into all the jihad shit, pardon my French --- but now he knows he didn't. We've made sure he's seen very graphic images of what his co-conspirators did --- and it sickens him.

"What I'm saying is that we may very soon have the keys to the terrorists dark Internet."

"And until then," Porter asked,

"In its original form, The Program had built-in safeguards to keep the names of American citizens hidden even from you --- without a legitimate court order. We could reinstate those protocols in such a way that they couldn't be removed without disabling the whole thing. If we do that, given this sudden change of climate, I think we could get the support of the courts and of the intelligence community in Congress.

"No," Porter said. "We all trust ourselves to do the right thing now --- but do any of you want this kind of power in the hands of people in the future we don't know and have no way of controlling. Remember, ultimate power corrupts ultimately. Let's not go there. Find another way."

The news for the next couple of weeks was dominated by coverage of the different attacks across the country and the F.B.I., local and state police raiding the homes of killed, wounded, or arrested perpetrators. What was unusual this time was the lack of, "Oh, he was such a nice, quiet, young man who kept to himself." More and more neighbors and acquaintances willingly offered insights and observations into the lives and backgrounds of the attackers.

The President was getting a lot of heat but true to his word, he wouldn't allow any member of his team to be sacrificed. He did more interviews in the first week than he'd done since taking office. The result was that the country saw a President they believed.

Barely making even the local news were stories about sites known to be training camps set up inside the U.S. These locations were raided, computers confiscated, suspects arrested, buildings and facilities burned or demolished by bulldozers and backhoes. The story of such a camp just across the U.S. border in Mexico was reported as just another drug cartel bust. What was really happening was with the specific okay from the President, all known potential threat sites were being eliminated.

Also off the media radar for the most part was the fact that President Randall spent two and a half days almost constantly on the telephone to the families of victims. The President's sympathy and compassion clearly made a connection with everyone with whom he spoke. The hardest calls were to those in the military who thought they were in the worst danger being deployed overseas of anyone in their family only to learn of the injury or death of a loved one back home. This, of course, took its toll on Porter. He went to bed each night drained but getting the understanding and support he needed from Deidra and his daughter, Page, by phone and from sister, Irene in person.

The upcoming Congressional Elections were coming to a head as a background to all of this tragedy. The second Tuesday in August was the date of the actual election. When the votes were tallied, it was clearly a victory for the President although he chose to see it as a victory for the American electorate. The newly elected congress members were to take their seats on October 1st.

CHAPTER 39

Graham Newcome brought Porter a list of potential candidates for the Associate Justice position on the Supreme Court a week after the Congressional Election. After carefully studying the resumes the President selected Karie Ann Cantu, Chief Judge of the Idaho Court of Appeals as the judge he wanted to talk to.

Mrs. Cantu had been a juvenile public defender for a dozen years after graduating from the University of Michigan Law School in Ann Arbor. Next she moved to the Shoshone county district attorney's office as a prosecutor for the next fifteen years. She became Idaho Attorney General for six years and was appointed Chief Judge of the state's Court of Appeals two years ago.

The average height, Rubenesque, sixty-one year old, with only a few streaks of grey in her otherwise, raven black hair, had a rose colored birth mark on her neck below her right jaw. Black horn rimmed glasses hung on a chain around her neck and rested on her ample bosom. She was dressed in a deep purple suit and wore a natural smile that crinkled the laugh lines around her penetrating eyes.

"Nice place you have here," she said looking around as she sat on one of the couches across from Porter who was joined by the Vice President, his Chief-of-Staff, the Director of White House Communications, and brother-in-law advisor Mark Meehan.

"It makes a good first impression," Porter said.

"But looks can be deceiving," Judge Cantu observed getting his meaning.

"Exactly," he said.

"That's the reputation of the whole town."

"It's a good place to have a dog," Porter said.

"Or a spouse," Vice President Ives said.

"Isn't that the plan?" the Judge said cutting her eyes to Porter.

"I wish we could just run off to Vegas," the President said.

"Does she know what she's getting into?" Cantu seemed to be well aware of what the world of Washington, D.C. involved.

"My wife," Mark spoke up, "his sister," motioning to Porter with his head, "has given her the 'full disclosure' talk."

The judge had a good, deep laugh.

"What do you think of the job we're talking to you about?" Porter cut right to it.

"Not a whole lot," she said. "It's never been an ambition of mine --- even in my weaker moments."

"But you made the trip to check it out," Cinnamon said.

"It would have been rude not to --- especially given the fact that I didn't say 'No' when I was first contacted."

"So you are at least interested?" Porter said.

"Interested, Mr. President, only because of how our justice system works. I've not always been pleased with what comes down from the Supreme Court. And I'm well aware that no one makes significant changes here from out in Idaho."

"Your vote on anything would be only one of nine," Porter said.

"I've got that. And, by the way, I think you were right to promote from within to the Chief Justice position. I would never have considered that job."

"Why not?

"My current position is as a Chief Judge. I know what it's like to come in from the outside and assume leadership nobody believes you've earned."

"Then you would consider this job?"

"Oh, I've been considering it since I got the first call. My husband and I have had some very involved discussions about it."

"What's his position, if I may ask?" Graham entered the conversation for the first time.

"He'll support me whatever I decide --- and he wants me to decide. We have no children so our careers have been pretty much our lives. He's going to retire next year or the year after and he's willing to do whatever I want."

"This is a lifetime appointment," Mark said.

"We know," the Judge said.

"Your honor," Porter said after a moment, "we have been impressed with your record over the years. You make good decisions --- according to either the spirit or the letter of the law depending on the case."

"I've never been one who believes that lawmakers are without flaw and neither are laws --- no matter how carefully or sloppily they are crafted. Even once a bill becomes the law, regardless of how deeply it might be carved in stone --- times change, circumstances have a tremendous impact on events --- and most importantly there's the human element."

"That's the kind of thinking I have been looking for, Judge."

"You've not ask me anything about my politics."

"Your heart and your mind are the main criteria for this job as far as I'm concerned."

"With that as our understanding, Mr. President, then I am definitely interested."

"Then can you tell us about your philosophy of the law?" the President asked sitting back.

"There's this ol' saw called the Constitution I really like," Judge Cantu said. "I don't believe it is the *'be all and end all'* of legal or political thought --- but it's a sight better than anything else I've come across --- and believe me, I've looked.

"I am afraid of my government --- the Executive Branch, the Legislative Branch, and the Judicial Branch. I have a concealed-carry gun permit and --- except for today --- I am always armed. I have a strong affinity for the Second Amendment --- I also understand the inherent dangers of an armed citizenry. But I see guns a lot like knives and cars. Knives and cars don't kill --- people do. A drunk, a crazy, and a bully with a badge is just as liable to do damage with a knife or a car as with a gun. I wouldn't mind if my government were afraid of me. I believe that's what those who drafted the Constitution wanted. Such a government would be less corrupt and more likely to listen to its citizens."

"Is the Second Amendment your favorite?" the President asked almost with a smile.

"No. I'm kind of partial to all items in the Bill of Rights --- but I do think the Tenth Amendment is the most overlooked of them all. Its twenty-eight words are very inconvenient to people and organizations with power."

Judge Cantu quoted the amendment from memory, "The powers not delegated to the United States by the Constitution, nor prohibited by it to the States, are reserved to the States respectively, or to the people."

"And what exactly does this mean to you?" Porter asked.

"That the states are each smaller versions of the whole country --- that each is a working experiment in democracy --- just as the counties, towns and cities are within a state. Just as there are wet and dry counties, I believe in the individual and even smaller collective will of the people.

"I'm no fan of the new rights that courts have discovered in the Constitution --- rights which are not and never were there. In the denomination, The Disciples of Christ, The Christian Church, we have a saying --- 'Where the scriptures speaks, we speak. Where the scriptures are silent we are silent.' I have the same view of the Constitution --- if it's not there, clearly spelled out in simple, plain English --- it's none of the courts business."

Porter looked around the room before he said, "I believe we have our candidate."

CHAPTER 40

There was a breath of relief in the media and by extension the nation when Saturday the fifth of September approached. The White House wedding of President Porter Randall to Deidra McAffie was characterized as everything from "Second Time Around" to "Murphy's Romance" and even "The Philadelphia Story." Any leak about arrangements, colors, flowers, bride's and groom's cakes were considered scoops. Naturally any information about the bride's gown was golden, but that data was all but Top Secret. The only disclosure was that both Deidra's gown and going-away dress were designed by an unnamed Texas designer.

An invitation to the white tie event was the most coveted ticket in Washington. Back stories of both the President and his soon-to-be new First Lady were the talk of gossip TV and the Internet.

Page, Porter's daughter, took time off her medical practice and flew in from Lubbock after two wedding showers for Deidra were held, one in Amarillo and the other in Canyon outside Deidra's ranch. Porter got reports on the ladies' agenda for the upcoming day at supper each night from sister, Irene. Once Deidra arrived in town she was overwhelmed by the crowd at Dulles International Airport with people wanting just a glimpse of the President's fiancé in spite of all video footage suddenly available of the fifty year old, Chestnut haired, Texas beauty.

Besides the news of the war and the investigations of July terrorists attacks, each daily White House Press Briefing had at least one question about the approaching nuptials. Comedy sketches and actual video of wedding mishaps seemed to be all over TV and the Internet.

"We certainly didn't count on this," Cinnamon commented one day to the President. "But your wedding is giving the country an uplift in spirit."

"So, you're saying that if we changed our minds and did run off to Vegas …."

"You'd do more than disappoint a lot of people, Mr. President --- I think you'd actually piss them off."

"We certainly don't want to do that."

"Since you won't let us even tell you about the polls," Grant Yarbrough said, "allow me to at least tell you we can use the boost."

"Those who live by the polls ---," the President began.

"Die by the polls?" his Press Secretary asked trying to finish the thought.

"No," Porter said with a wink, "I was going to say they live next to Germany and the Czech Republic."

The pun got the laugh the President wanted.

"A prospective groom with a sense of humor," Porter's brother-in-law added stepping up to the group. "Make sure you hang on to that. You're going to need it."

"Is there something specific?" the President asked.

"No. Merely sage advice from an old married man."

"One of biggest joys is making Deidra laugh." Then after a pause, Porter asked, "Am I the only one with a job around here?"

"Humor us," Mark Meehan said. "We could always tell the press where you're going for your honeymoon."

"That's playing dirty. Blackmail even."

"Tomayto --- tomahto," the President's chief advisor joked.

"There is this," Graham Newcome walked up and said holding up a telephone note. "Most likely the last act of the old House as we knew it. They've passed the water recovery aquifer recharge bill. Felix Alvarez delivered as promised."

"Alvarez? The lawyer?" Cinnamon asked. "I didn't know we were working with him."

"We weren't," Porter said, "--- at least not until now. He said he could deliver on this --- it was a kind of test."

"I'd say he passed," Mark said.

The Press Secretary said, "I've only heard rumors of Mr. Alvarez. They must be true."

"And we have him in our corner now," the President said.

The group broke up and went about their business.

The very few moments Porter and Deidra had together were precious and spent more in silence than in conversation. After all they had said so much to each other over the years, not much had gone unsaid. The few kisses they shared were like undiscovered stars. They warmed them both and filled them with an inner glow everyone could see.

On the evening of the wedding the White House was resplendent in flowers, bows, candles and gleaming, polished wood and music from an orchestra set up in the State Dining Room which filtered through the halls. The ceremony took place in the East Room. The chairs were divided by an aisle down the elegant chamber from the cross hallway. A rough wooden arch two steps up on a platform was decorated with the bride's colors, cranberry and evergreen.

Porter entered from the south door from the Green Room with the minister from the New York Avenue Presbyterian Church in D.C. wearing a purple stole with white and gold stitching. Porter wore a cranberry colored lapel boutonniere on his long tailed black coat.

Many attendees looked at one another wondering what the music was when the orchestra began playing the love theme from the film,

Dune. Porter had to bite his lip to keep from smiling. He knew that coming down the stairs Deidra was hearing the same melody and thinking, as he was, "the sleepers have awoken."

Three bride's maids came down the aisle, two close friends of Deidra and Cinnamon Higdon, each escorted by friends of Porter's. Each lady wore a beautiful floor length, empire waist, cranberry dress. The maid of honor was Porter's obviously pregnant daughter, Page, was ushered in by best man, brother-in-law Mark Meehan. When the last pair took up their positions, the orchestra ended the previous piece, almost magically. All eyes then turned to the door as the wedding march sounded.

Deidra entered alone wearing an elegant cream colored bridal gown and sweeping train. The entire dress was accented by beads of pearls leading up to a shoulder less bodice, covered by a lovely veil flowing down with her shiny chestnut shoulder length hair from a pearl tiara. The room collectively caught its breath at the beautiful image of the bride as she seemed to glide to the awaiting President.

The ceremony, like most Protestant weddings, was brief. After the pair exchanged rings and Porter lifted Deidra's veil, he took her in his arms for a kiss that became the image of the wedding to the world.

The reception filed through the oval shaped Blue Room. It was hours later, after a wedding dinner on the South Lawn under a white covered awning, when Porter got a chance to dance with his sister. He said, "You did a wonderful job of this."

"Had some pretty good help."

"And I know you all enjoyed every moment of it?"

"How many get a chance to plan a White House wedding?"

"Thanks for playing the mother-of-the-bride."

"Never got to do it for any kids of my own. So I loved it. Best of all, I am so happy to see you and Deidra together. We all wondered how long it was going to take before you two figured out what everybody else knew years ago?"

"The sleepers have awoken."

"Yes." Then his sister's eyes lit up. "Dune. That was the last piece of music before the wedding march."

"We didn't think anybody would figure that out."

"I'll bet Mark got it, too. He loves that movie. I don't know how many times we've seen it."

"I should have known. Rocket scientist --- science fiction."

"Now, for the next two weeks, leave everything to your people here. You have an excellent team. This time should be for you and Deidra."

"I hope it can be --- unfortunately, somethings are going to have to be up to me."

"I know. But as much as you can, focus on your bride."

"Yes, mother," Porter smiled.

CHAPTER 41

The newlyweds were under the media's radar for little over a half a day. Media was caught off guard when word leaked out that Air Force One was hidden in a hangar at what the locals still called Elmendorf Air Force Base in Anchorage --- officially Joint Base Elmendorf-Richardson --- Fort Richardson, the Army post, and Elmendorf were merged in 2010.

The presence of the gigantic Lockheed/Martin C-5A Galaxy should have drawn attention first since it sat out in the open on the tarmac. But planes like this one which held the President's limo convoy and a folded up Marine One were no stranger in Anchorage skies or the base's runways.

Shortly after touching down, Marine One was unpacked and the first couple lifted into clouds to a destination which remained secret for a few days longer. The President and new First Lady were spending their honeymoon at a plush, private Alaskan Mountain Range retreat owned by Porter's publisher --- and even financed, in part, by the company's profits from Porter's novels --- profits which had increased significantly since his becoming President.

The log cabin motif was just that --- a style more than a reality. Solar panels on the roof and a strategically placed wind turban in a mountain pass less than a mile away insured all the power the main lodge or any of the other three cabins could ever need. A live-in staff took care of the property as well as served as cooks and guides as needed.

Deidra and Porter enjoyed fly fishing in one of the Chulitna Rivers. There are two of them in the state --- the one they used was a seventy mile long tributary to the Susitna River which emptied into Cook Outlet where Captain James Cook sailed in his 1778 expedition in search of the Northwest Passage. Anchorage was just that, an anchorage for Cook and later the manager of the Russian American trading company, Alexander Baranov, when Russia owned the forty-ninth state.

The Secret Service set up a headquarters in one of the other cabins and accompanied the First Couple on their outings on foot, horseback, or by Marine One. It was a beautiful setting with magnificent Mt. McKinley almost always in view. After a week the President summoned White House Photographer, Leigh Janda, to take some stills and even video footage for the sake of history and the current day media. One shot which proved to be the most captivating to the press was of Deidra and Porter eating M.R.E.s in the snow on a glacier with the beautiful mountains behind them. Another memorable picture was the First Couple cuddling with cups of coffee on the front porch of the main cabin at sunset.

Both the President and the First Lady expected their two weeks alone together to be cut short --- and it was two days after their first week. While they were both secretly expecting some national crisis or incident relating to the war, the event was a whistle blower who exposed corrupt and politically motivated funding within the Department of Education.

What had become a common practice in the D.O.E. was selectively rewarding districts which had supported the previous administration while subtly punishing districts and whole states which were considered politically adversaries. According to the leaked documents, the practice had been going on under several administrations, including the last two. That it was still occurring under Porter's watch was a flashpoint.

On the flight back to D.C., Porter notified both his Chief-of-Staff and called the Secretary of Education, Francene Tepler. To both of them the President made it abundantly clear that nothing had better happen to the whistle blower, a Ph.D. staffer named Regis Yablonski. The President had Graham Newcome dispatch Secret Service agents to Yablonski to insure his and his family's health. There was only a Mrs. Yablonski, their children were all grown and living across the country. Graham sent an agent to each and saw that Dr. Yablonski and his wife were installed in a comfortable hotel with around the clock security.

At Andrews A.F.B. in Washington, the First Couple was welcomed by a throng of media and the public. Deidra's heart shaped face was all smiles, and she held on to Porter's arm as they descended the steps from Air Force One. To one reporter's question as the President and First Lady crossed the lawn from Marine One to the White House, "How was the honeymoon?" Porter answered, "Not long enough."

As expected one late night comic played the clip and added, "That's what she said." It got a big laugh and the President admitted he walked into that one.

Irene awaited Deidra and they disappeared upstairs in the East Wing while the President gathered the Vice President, Graham, Mark, Cinnamon, and Grant in the Oval office for a quick conference. After getting the latest details Porter said, "I think we need to meet Dr. Yablonski."

"Mrs. Jacobs has him on your schedule at three this afternoon," Graham said.

"What can you tell me about him?"

"He was a high school chemistry teacher in Nebraska," Vice President Sundee Ives said, "who went back and got both his Masters and Ph.D. He was an assistant principal, principal and superintendent before he was invited to join the Department of Education."

"He's not a big talker," Cinnamon said. "But when he does say something, it's important."

"He is well liked by people who have worked with him at every level --- but he's not an assertive person," Mark said. "He must have tried and tried to get someone up the line to listen to him about this favoritism --- and when no one would --- he spoke up."

"How's he standing up to all the attention?" Porter asked.

"I'd say better than even he expected," Chief-of-Staff Graham Newcome said. "How could anybody be ready for what being a whistle blower brings down on you?"

"Some of the media outlets are looking under every leaf and stone to find some dirt on him," Press Secretary Grant Yarbrough said. "So far they've found nothing."

"What he needs is a bulldog --- someone to speak up for him and let him know he's not alone."

"You can do the last part when you see him, Mr. President," said Porter's pretty White House Communications Director.

"I will," he said.

"And I think I know someone who can be his bulldog," Cinnamon continued. "She went to law school with me --- and she works in the Justice Department. Once she gets her teeth into something --- well, I've yet to see her bite off more than she could chew and spit out."

"Get her," Porter said. "The Attorney General doesn't know it yet, but he just assigned her to Dr. Yablonski. And what's her name?"

"Battles. Bethany Jane Battles."

"Tell her," Porter said in his best TV gameshow hosting voice, "to *come on down.*"

CHAPTER 42

The political races always heated up prior to the national conventions in mid to late summer of an election year. There was no law, but tradition since 1952 had dictated that the party out of power would hold their convention first and the incumbent party second. Since Porter was a declared Independent, this could have caused some problems. Additionally given the fact that he was finishing the term of a Democrat, Leo Gibson, and had retained a majority of Gibson appointments, it could be argued that the Democrats were the incumbent party. But the Republican's conceded that the President had caucused with them when he was in Congress. They took the second slot.

On the Democratic side a large group of potential candidates had emerged. The clear leader was Senator George Tossen from California, the Democratic Senate Majority Leader. Two current cabinet members under Randall had joined the fray --- Attorney General Winchell Hardwick, and Francene Tepler the Secretary of Education. Three sitting Democratic governors and one former governor also added their name to the roster. The rest of the field was made up of two members of the House of Representatives, one TV political talk show hostess, a college professor of political science and three business men. Of the total of fourteen declared candidates, all were male except for two --- one current governor and the TV personality. Three were black and two were Hispanic.

Vice President Sundee Ives was pressed to run but she declined unequivocally. Having served as Acting President for the months Porter was in a coma had given the former New Hampshire governor all of the oval office she wanted. Even Dr. Clara Sonnenberg, the fifty year old Secretary of State declined offers of support. Political commentators bemoaned the loss of these two strong and respected women from the field of candidates.

Senator Tossen was the most credentialed and experienced of the Democratic field plus he had name recognition. In the early going he took a commanding lead. But the Majority Leader, wheelchair bound due to a diving accident as a teenager, always seemed to photograph as being distant and elite. He was rarely bombastic but logical and clear spoken. His political team had always tried to make Tossen appear to be a modern day F.D.R.

For the Republican side it would have seemed the ideal year for all comers. The list of possible candidates was, however, limited to only eight. Naturally, Speaker of the House, Vincent Sturges, the sixty-three year old venerable statesman, with bushy eye brows and a full shock of ice white hair was in the race from the outset. So was his political rival in the House, the wiry, Majority Whip, Tray Rifkin, Representative from Arizona. The forty-four year old rancher/wine grower was seen as a voice for causes often considered too liberal for many in the Grand Old Party. His characteristic white Stetson always made him easy to pick out of any line up of candidates.

A wealthy stock fund manager, two self-made business tycoons, one a woman, one a Hispanic man, added their names to the roll. The field was rounded out by an attractive 40 year-old conservative author, blogger and popular TV guest commentator, a black former New York mayor, and a former N.F.L. quarterback who was governor of Nebraska.

The platforms for the different candidates were pinned to single issues in both parties, and the challenge was how to conduct a campaign with a popular incumbent President. Of course there was the liberal anti-war theme but it didn't play very well with a public twice assaulted at home by terrorists.

Attempts to divide the electorate by class, income, and race became the single uniting signatory of the Democrats and were promising more entitlements and soak-the-rich taxes. The Republicans had their evangelical and right-to-life constituents along with the self-defense Second Amendment groups.

It seemed each party was talking to those already committed to them instead of trying to widen their reach to the independents who were clearly going to be the swing voters.

The President's Balanced Budget Amendment was gathering strength as the new members of Congress took their seats. Those who decried it were often slowed down by their own leadership. The common sense of the concepts had taken profound hold in the country.

Porter stayed out of the political skirmishing and had Press Secretary Grant Yarbrough issue a standard "no comment" to questions designed to draw him into the party politics. Grant had a fun couple of hours when he met with Cinnamon Higdon and Head Speech Writer, Therese Herzog, to come up with some different way of saying "no comment."

"I'll say 'Bite me" if I have too."

"Grant," Cinnamon said, "we can't be that blunt."

"How about the ol' 'How do know politicians are lying? Their lips are moving,'" the speech writer offered.

"That's a better way to go," the White House Communications Director said.

"Then, how about, 'The White House doesn't have a dog in this fight'?"

"Good."

"We could also say, 'Our jobs here are governing. It's the professional politicians' jobs to tell you what they think you want to hear.'"

"Another good one," Cinnamon smiled.

"You're good at this, Therese," Grant said.

It was the first time she ever felt he was even aware she was in the room. She felt herself blushing.

"We need to be thinking like the President. What might he say if asked about something in the political battle between the Democrats and the Republicans?" Cinnamon wanted to keep the conversation on track.

"I try to hear his voice when I write for him," Therese said.

"Then this might work, 'Ask that question again *after* you've posed it to the candidates,'" the Press Secretary suggested.

"Or," Theresa said, "'Ask not for whom the bell tolls on this --- it tolls for you.'"

"Whoa! I think I'll just shut up and listen," Grant said.

"Come on, Grant," Cinnamon smiled, "you've been on the air --- live --- you're used to thinking on your feet."

"Okay," Grant sat forward, "I could say, 'The difference between those running to get in this office and those who are here now is the difference between fact and fiction.'"

"Now you're talking," Cinnamon said.

"Yes," Theresa agreed.

CHAPTER 43

Irene absolutely refused to stay in the White House. Porter made the argument that there were plenty of bedrooms but she was firm.

"Two women can't run the same house --- especially this one. And besides, you two are newly married. You do *not* need anyone else around."

In the end he convinced her to move into Blair House. "You and Mark are doing me a favor, Sis. Don't forget that."

"And Mark's getting a paycheck."

"But you're not. Come one, Blair House is just across the street."

"Tell you what," she said. "We'll stay in Trowbridge House --- you can still have your secret meeting there if you need to ---."

"How'd you know...."

"Pillow talk. I'm sleeping with your chief advisor. And if you have guests --- and Presidents do have that from time to time --- they can still have Blair House."

"Okay, okay," he threw up his hands. "But we still have family dinners."

"A couple of times a week at the most."

"You drive a hard bargain, Sis."

Dr. Regis Yablonski was a shy little man with a bulbous nose which held his trifocal glasses at a slight angle on his freckled face. His tiny, flat chested wife, Loreena, held tightly on to his arm. It almost seemed that it took the both of them to make one complete person. She never said a word but exchanged glances with her husband from time to time, always looking completely supportive.

"Dr. and Mrs. Yablonski," the President said, "this is Ms. Bethany Jane Battles. Will you please give her a dollar?"

The Yablonskies were caught off guard by the request, but with his wife's nod, he reached into his pants pocket and pulled out some change. He counted out three quarters, two dimes and a nickel.

"Thank you," the equally petite but fashion model pretty thirty-five year old woman said putting the change in the side pocket of her stylish suit.

"Ms. Battle works for the Department of Justice, but as of this moment, you have hired her as your personal attorney. Anything you say to her is covered by attorney/client privilege. She is one-hundred percent on your side. If it comes to a question you or the D.O.J. --- you win. Understand?"

The couple nodded their heads while looking each other in the eye.

"Everyone, please have a seat," Porter said to all, including his Chief-of-Staff, Director of White House Communications, and his brother-in-law advisor.

"You're a brave man, Dr. Yablonski," Porter said when everyone was comfortable.

"No, sir, I'm not," the educator said. "But there comes a time …." He couldn't finish the thought.

"I understand. But it's what you do when you reach that point that defines bravery from cowardice. You, sir, are a brave man. I intend to see that you get all the support you need."

For the first time, Mrs. Yablonski smiled.

"Ms. Battle is going to set up a special investigative committee over at Justice. I want you to head it, but she will be your voice. She will convene the meetings, ask the questions and see that the truth will out. With your help she will select some people you believe are honest in your department to sit on that committee. They together with you will decide who to call as witnesses, and you will have complete access to any and all papers, e-mail, records --- whatever you need. Ms. Battle as lead council will conduct the questioning of witnesses and if you two feel some sessions need to be closed-door --- you call it and that's the way it will be.

"Now at the end of this," Porter went on after everyone grasped all he had just said, "there are going to be some people fired and maybe some will even go to jail. You, Dr. Yablonski, are going to be the example to others all across our government of what is possible when you stick by your principals and call out those who are misusing the power of the federal government.

"Do you have any questions?"

The Yablonskies didn't.

"Ms. Battle, do you?"

"No, Sir," she said confidently.

"Reports about your meeting are not to go up the chain of command at the Justice Department but are to be marked 'Eyes Only' and come directly to me. Let's see if we can't make government work for a change."

Porter's next meeting of the day was with Felix Alvarez the well-connected D.C. lawyer and deal maker who had kept his side of the test run of his abilities by getting Porter's aquifer measure through the House. The two men shook hands warmly before they sat across from each other on the couches in the Oval office. Graham Newcome, who had recommended Alvarez to begin with, and advisor Mark Meehan sat with Porter.

"Am I asking to look behind the curtain if I ask how you pulled this off?" Porter asked.

"I would love to say there was some magic involved and that I'm some sort of Hogwarts Wizard," the short dark skinned attorney laughed, "but the truth is, Mr. President, that I count on the better angels in people's natures --- and am rarely disappointed."

"But Vincent Sturges just barely won his seat back."

"Because he is an honest man. He's not one of those who have gotten rich out of being in public office. What seems like *his* money all came from his wife --- who inherited it on the death of her father --- legitimately. Vincent has made sure it has stayed in her name, incidentally.

"I'm surprised because he was so angry with me when I first stepped into this office."

"Oh, Vincent has a short fuse --- but he's also the kind of guy who blows up and it all blows over. He says, 'I apologize --- I was out of line' more than anyone else I've ever known. And his word, which he gave to you, is his bond."

"Then I need to call him and say, 'Thank you, can we be friends?'"

"Do that," Alvarez said, "but also think about inviting all the new elected members of Congress over for --- a get together of some sort . Including those who were able to keep their seats."

"Isn't it a bit late to be doing that now?"

"It's never too late."

"You're right, Mr. Alvarez. How about a conversation in the East Room?" Graham suggested.

"And some Texas bar-b-cue on the lawn afterwards?" Mark said.

"Done," Porter said. "And Mr. Alvarez, can I get you to join my staff?"

"If you'll call me Felix. Mr. Alvarez was my dad."

CHAPTER 44

The East Room was crowded with members of both houses of Congress. When the President entered, it was through the same door he'd used when he made his appearance for his wedding. This time he took the steps of a riser and stepped up to the podium with the Presidential Seal in front. Everyone rose to strains of "Hail To The Chief," played by an abbreviated version of the Marine Band.

"Please be seated," Porter said and everyone followed his instructions.

The President looked around the room, up at the windows and the three chandeliers hanging from the ceiling.

"The last time I was in this room, I only got to say a couple of words." This got a chuckle from his audience. "And you'll be glad to know I don't have many to say, today." There was even scattered applause and a little more laughter.

"While you, the Legislative Branch, my team and I, the Executive Branch, have different functions --- I hope we don't have to be at cross purposes --- and I hope we're not. You more closely represent the people who sent you here than I do --- I get that. Our joint purpose should however be to do the best and be the best we can be for the American public."

Porter looked down at the notes and looked up with a bit of a smile.

"By definition, politics is the art of compromise --- give and take. Let's do that --- see where we can come together. Let's not be as Reagan described politics as '...the second oldest profession.' One which he said, "...bears a striking resemblance to the first.'"

This lightened the mood of the room.

After a moment, Porter went on, "We know there are those who wish to utterly destroy our way of life, our freedoms, and our ability to defend ourselves. My watch is short, but I do not intend to see any of that happen while I am President.

"One of the issues which brought you all here to Washington, I hope, was, first, the public to demand greater accountability from our government. This was what got you elected --- or reelected --- your pledge to do just that. We have men and women right this very moment fighting and dying for our rights and for us to have a government which serves them, represents them --- a government which is supposed to be fair and just to us all.

"The legislation I asked Congress for in my first State of the Nation address was number one — the Term Limits on service in Congress --- to limit the terms of members of Congress may service just as we have limited those of any President --- to eliminate Congressional tenure --- to make your branch of our government accountable to the people by having Congress live by the same rules and regulations it stipulates for everyone else --- to end Congressional pay and benefits when a member's term ends --- and to make Congressional retirement either Social Security or self-purchased retirement and Congressional health care — the same one you legislate for the public.

"The greatest thing George Washington did was to set the example of giving up power, stepping aside, before the allure, the corruption of power could taint his actions, his goals, and his name. Are you strong enough to do this, too?

"Are you wise enough to demand that the legislators who will come after you will live by the same laws they make for all the rest of us? Are you brave enough to align your pay and benefits with those who are in uniform serving our country? Do you dare do what you were elected to do? And most importantly, do you have the will?

"Secondly, the Balanced Budget Amendment. If we can't balance our national budget and pay our bills --- we can't do anything else. These C.R.'S — Continuing Resolutions to keep kicking the can and hard work on a real budget — must stop. It has been years since we last had a budget — a balanced budget. No one can live their daily life — no company can operated without one. Neither can our nation.

"Remember your campaign promises and pledges.

"We are currently dealing with the immoral effects the coils of power have had on some in our Department of Education. It is all around us --- just waiting to be exposed. This town is more renowned for its corruption than for fairness, honesty, and justice. What a sad commentary this is on us all --- and I include myself in this as well. None of us are beyond our laws.

"All I can tell you is that I am doing my very best to be who our nation needs at this time. I ask you to be a part of that army, too. I don't ask you to agree with me but only that you do what you know in your heart is right, correct, evenhanded, and honorable.

"Again, Reagan once said, 'The nearest thing to eternal life we will ever see on this earth is a government program.'"

The legislators couldn't help but laugh at this remark.

"I say, the business of our nation is *not* government. The business of America is 'life, liberty, and the pursuit of happiness.' Help our people live productive, creative, satisfying and fulfilling lives --- free from the burden of being over-taxed and over-regulated. This is a huge task. In order to accomplish it, I ask that you reclaim your Constitutional rights to legislate and remove much of the regulative power Congress has in the past given over to the Executive Branch."

This remark produced applause from the audience.

"Lastly, I challenge you not to do what has become common practice for members of Congress --- namely to spend seventy to ninety percent of your time fund raising for your next election --- and to then serve those who support you financially. Thirty percent or less of your time spent in actually legislating is a shameful exercise of what you were elected to do.

"Please be the best you, you were elected to be," Porter began wrapping up, "Give that person within you the strength and the resolve to be that person in everything you to do --- everything you say --- everything for which you will cast your vote for or against. Then that person will shine through your every pore, and you will accomplish greater things than you have ever imagined."

The President let those words ring across the room before he said, "Now, let me meet you --- and let's eat!"

CHAPTER 45

The war continued to go well. ISIS, the Taliban, Al-Qaeda, Boko Haram, and the other splinter terrorists groups were all but wiped out every time they dared to stand and fight. They continued to try to vanish into the local population which made it a house to house fight many times. But this time, with an administration that understood the tactic and who allowed the military to conduct the fight as they needed to, the outcome was becoming increasingly a one sided fight. The other N.A.T.O. and allied countries followed the U.S. lead, and cells both large and small were being crushed and eliminated.

The Chinese were trying to stabilize their economy which was showing signs of crumbling because of its own devastating internal corruption and overbearing government. Russia wanted to take advantage of the American focus elsewhere, but attempts to make moves in the Baltic were met with such resistance that the bear was rethinking its options.

A late season hurricane struck from the Gulf of Mexico in Texas and the slow moving storm smashed into a Canadian cold front as the remnants of the downgraded tropical system reached the U.S. heartland bringing flooding to the upper Mississippi Valley. The flooding grew as it spread downstream.

National Guard, F.E.M.A. (Federal Emergency Management Agency), and the Red Cross surged into action but the devastating effects of the flood waters made a powerful impact on the nation. Help came from across the country --- fireman, policeman, truckers, and ordinary citizens were drawn to the site, and the media coverage proved to be predominately positive because of the outpouring of the American willingness to help.

President Randall and the First Lady toured the hardest hit area in Air Force One and then by local helicopter --- stopping to meet governors, mayors and suffering citizens. What most impressed the President was the resilient spirit of the people they met.

"We've got this, Mr. President," one man from New Mexico said unloading the flat bottom fishing boat he'd towed from home to the flood. "I look at it like God has made me a 'fisher of men.' You keep doing your job and we'll take care of these folks." It became a widely played soundbite on the networks and the Internet.

A woman from Pennsylvania serving meals in a high school gym told Deidra, "My son's fighting in the Middle East --- I thought I could help here in the Midwest. It's only fair."

In Missouri a flooded out farmer standing on a ledge looking out across his underwater fields told a reporter, "Next time I pray for rain --- think I'll be a little more specific about what I'm askin' for. We need to get this too much of a good thing out of here. There are people who need my crops."

Porter addressed a hasty impromptu press conference in Illinois, "God has truly blessed America. Okay, with too much rain, I grant you, but the overflowing of the milk of human kindness is truly America at its best."

"If I believed in God, I say Porter Randall was protected by a higher power," Deliah Rome the 35 year-old former White House Director of Communications under President Gibson said. The attractive, stylishly dressed woman was in a villa in Argentina meeting with Yale

Gallagher, the billionaire behind what was originally called the Watergate Group. That group of former Gibson administration power brokers had split up and disappeared the day after former member Victor Chesterfield had been named as the new Secretary of Defense.

She sat in a chair across from the pear shaped seventy year-old, rarely photographed albino with a tiny mouth and large ears. He wore a light blue Irish linen guayabera or Mexican banker's shirt and dark slacks. His polished Italian leather shoes reflected the sunlight from the decoratively wrought iron barred windows. Deliah let the split in her skirt ride up high on her thigh exposing more of her shapely legs than was needed.

"But you're not a believer," Gallagher said, "and neither am I. So how do we explain his Teflon veneer?"

"I wish I knew. I'd rip it off and expose him in an instant if I could."

"What if what's underneath isn't what you expect?"

"Meaning?"

"In my life I'm met some people who are --- called lucky, blessed, or providential --- but they seem to be the right person in the right place at the right time --- and no one can explain it. I've taken down a few of them in my day --- but they always seem to rise out of the ashes. That could be the kind of person we're dealing with here."

"You'll excuse me if I don't buy into it. From my experience, everyone is a fool, a sucker, a pervert even. All you need is to find the right opening --- the right bait."

"Is that what you think of me, Deliah?" the old man asked narrowing his eyes.

She reached across and placed a soft hand on one of his knees.

"Shared perversion is a shared delight, Yale. Consenting adults and all that. We're not trying to make anyone believe we're anything else."

"Unless it's to our advantage."

"Well, of course," she winked and sat back.

"Do you have a plan for getting to Randall?" he asked a moment later.

"That's why I'm here."

"You need financing for your idea?"

"I need a co-conspirator," she said. "All the rest of my band of warriors are all hiding and huddling in little holes somewhere. To get to Randall will take contrivance, guile, trusted confederates, and boldness."

"I thought we tried that in Milwaukee."

"Yes, but if at first you don't succeed…."

"What do you suggest?"

"First of all, I think we should take it to bed and think about it. There is a magic time between orgasm and sleep where sometimes sparks of brilliance come to us."

CHAPTER 46

Before dawn the morning of Christmas Eve, Air Force One touched down at Nnamdi Azikiwe International Airport in Nigeria. From there President Randall took a CH-47 Chinook helicopter to fire support base, Daisy Duke.

The available troops had been mustered in the open garrison area and stood or sat in the heat complaining for about an hour before the double-roter chopper set down and the President stepped up onto the stage.

"At ease!" the President said wearing a camo baseball cap with the President's seal on it. Instantly the troops relaxed and cheered. "I bring you 4th of July — Independence Day greetings from a grateful nation!"

In the minutes that followed Porter told the men and women the only reason the First Lady wasn't here was because she was making a whirlwind trip to V.A. Hospitals back home.

This warmed the hearts of those listening to the President. Most of them knew someone stateside since they had been shot or injured. To know that the Commander-In-Chief and the First Lady were thinking of them touched them in a way most civilians would never understand.

"I have an M.R.E. with M&Ms," Porter said holding up an olive drab plastic bag with black printing on it. "Anybody want to trade?"

It was an inside joke only those who regularly ate the prepacked military rations would understand. Having M&M candies were worth the weight in gold of the rest of the meal and a prized trading option. The troops cheered and laughed. Here was a President who really understood life as they knew it.

What wasn't apparent was that the smell of canvas tents and cordite from firing howitzers was ingrained in Porter from his years in the service as a front line surgeon with M*A*S*H units in Iraq and Afghanistan. The smell always brought back vivid memories --- of blood and screaming as well as a deeply shared comradery with those who had served, sacrificed --- lived in constant fear of attack --- yet somehow found ways to laugh while passing days and nights of monotony interspersed with minutes and hours of surging adrenalin and absolute horror.

After about twenty minutes Porter said, "I wish I could stay and share a meal with you --- but *'I have miles to go before I sleep'* --- but I have a small present for each of you," he held up a Christmas wrapped box with ribbon and a bow big enough to hold a silver dollar. "I've left them with your commander.

"Thank you all for keeping us free!"

The scene was repeated five more times that day at different Western African bases. And again the same scenario played itself out the next two days in Jorden, Syria, Iraq, Iran, Pakistan and Afghanistan. Each soldier found in his or her little box, a Presidential Challenge Coin. It was the same thing Deidra was offering to those in V.A hospitals from New Hampshire to Florida, across the country to California and Oregon.

The First Lady's message was the same as Porter's --- you are not forgotten --- and the nation honors your service --- now and in the future.

Protesters against the war and against Porter's agenda were not as well attended as usually promised by protest leaders --- sometimes embarrassingly so. Americans seemed to have found their love for their country and its values much to the dismay and even anger of protesters who allowed their frustration to turn to violence. They were quickly arrested and the media was tepid it its support.

Having a President who sought to unite the country instead of dividing it was something new to younger Americans and to most of the media. Political commentary and political comedy found little to mock or dislike about this Accidental President. One comic had even asked is the nation should change the way we select our leaders?

A popular bumper sticker read, "Mom says I was an Accident. I told her so was the President." Intended as a slap at Porter, it had become a badge of honor for many supporters.

The Department of Education Investigation Panel became "must see TV" for most of the country. The feisty Bethany Jane Battles was a natural. Not only did the camera love her but soon so did the regular viewers of the broadcast hearings. The bright eyed, bob cut white blonde haired, obviously gorgeous attorney was penetrating with her questions, sarcastic when it was warranted, and so quick she would not let witnesses wiggle out of questions they'd rather not answer.

The surprising fact to the public was the number of government workers who knew what they were doing was wrong but who felt powerless to change procedures and policies dictated by their politically appointed bosses. It came out that there were some thoughtful, caring, honest people who had to keep their jobs to support their families and so felt coerced into actions they neither agreed with nor supported in the least.

When it was time for the policy makers to appear, all clung to their Fifth Amendment rights and consulted lawyers before giving any real answers. They were incriminating themselves through their evasive conduct and lack of moral compass, choosing to blame others higher up and sounding like Nazi henchmen at the Nuremberg Trials following World War II --- they were "just following orders."

Their superiors tried to stone wall Ms. Battle, which always proved to be a foolish and humiliating choice in the end. Others tried to claim their directives were misunderstood --- unable to defend their own word on memo and e-mails.

By the time the hearing ended in early February, the world knew Dr. Regis Yablonski was an honest man --- completely innocent of any wrong doing --- and a credit to himself and the nation. Porter fired six political appointees and complicit supervisors forcing his Attorney General, the spineless Winchell Hardwick, to bring federal charges against all and promote Ms. Bethany Jane Battles to be the chief prosecutor for all the cases. All but two plead guilty and got both heavy fines and some prison time.

The remaining two awaited their day in court with growing anxiety over what was to come.

The following week the President delivered a major address to the National Press Club in Washington concerning the Department of Education.

CHAPTER 47

The approaching November Presidential Election was the major news story of the day but often under the fold in newspapers and the third or fourth story in media newscasts. The dominate stories were (1) the war, (2) captured U.S. terrorists court cases, (3) the Department of Education scandal and then Presidential politics. Going to the National Press Club meant the President had to be prepared to take questions on all these topics --- he was, however, primarily invited to address the media professionals about the revelations, firings, and criminal charges brought as a result of the Special Investigation on the Department of Education --- and what the President's plans were moving forward.

The National Press Club had been the main tenant of 529 14th St. NW, since 1909. The building was almost sold to a Chinese corporation in 2015 but was saved at the last minute by a multi U.S. corporation deal which secured the landmark building only two blocks from the White House. There are more than 3,500 active members of the club which occupies primarily the thirteenth and fourteen floors --- one of the few American buildings having a thirteenth floor. Print, broadcast, and Internet journalists have office space throughout the structure along with legal firms, stocks and bond traders as well as a cross section of other D.C. business wanting to have a presence in the heart of the nation's capital.

Before arriving at the scheduled luncheon in the main conference room, Porter learned that the President was a member of the club --- all Presidents since Warren G. Harding had been. It was honorary. Porter told those who greeted him that he didn't believe in a free ride. He asked to be shown to the office of the Membership Chair. Inside the small office Porter pulled out his check book and wrote a check. The hallway was jammed with flashing and steady lights of digital still and video cameras.

"We'll use this picture in our next newsletter," the middle-aged woman said as images were snapped showing the President handing over his check. "This will be a nudge to our other members to pay up," she smiled.

Following the meal and his introduction, Porter stepped to the podium with the National Press Club stenciled background behind him. He pulled a small stack of cards from his inside coat pocket and put them down before he spoke.

"Since ancient time it's been noted, 'All that's needed for a school is a student, a teacher, and a log.' Can you imagine the environmental impact study such a log would require today?"

The anchors and reporters, camera operators couldn't help but laugh.

"This is where we are in education today. We focus on everything in the world that relates to the educational process --- we even have an entire federal government department to see to these matters --- the least of which turns out to be the important part.

"My mother was an elementary school teacher, my father a college professor. By the time they retired in frustration they both told me the very last thing they did with their time was teach. They advised anyone considering teaching to give plumbing and air conditioning work a fair consideration. Few understood them --- but some came back over the years and said it took them a while, but they finally got it.

"A group of anthropologists encountered a native tribe deep in the jungles of the South Pacific. These people had never been in contact with the outside world and even once the new comers learned enough of their language to communicate, there were still enormous gaps in their understanding of each other. When the scientists asked to meet the most important man in their male dominated village, they were taken to a clearing where an old man sat on a log surrounded by children.

"'No, no,' the anthropologists said. '"We want to meet your leader. Your chief.' 'Oh,' said the native, 'I thought you wanted to meet the most important man in our village. The chief is this way.'

"In our culture we put our money where our mouths --- our hearts --- our interests are. Can you imagine a school teacher getting a multi-million dollar contract --- a multi-year deal with built in bonuses --- like professional athletes or celebrities --- some celebrities whose only accomplishment in life is being famous?

"We give over our children, the next generation of Americans, five to eight hours a day to people whose names we really don't know and who we play less than those who pick up our garbage in some cities --- or what we'd have to pay all day babysitters. We then hog tie them to rules we would never and could never live by in our own homes with unruly, disobedient, rude, obnoxious, and even physically threatening children. What are we thinking?

"Then as a nation we have decided to pay taxes to the national government to do what we don't want to take the time to do ourselves --- understand what our children are to be taught --- by whom --- when --- where --- and under what conditions?"

As was his way, Porter let his words sink in before moving on.

"The investigation into our Department of Education shows us all what happens to funds we hand over to the government and to unknown and unaccountable bureaucrats who could never do what the average teacher does every day.

"What has happened to American education? First of all we have ranked actual teaching as the least important duty of a teacher. And if a teacher happens to excel at teaching --- the first thing we do is to pay them more money to leave the classroom --- to become an administrator --- and then a consultant --- and finally a teaching expert who works not with students or even other teachers but with bureaucrats.

"Our Department of Education is an example of what happens when we depend on the federal government to do what we as citizens --- as parents should be doing. If you take nothing away from here today, take this --- we have become a civilization dependent on Big Brother. We believe someone or some group --- some official organization --- knows what's best for not just our children, but for all of us. Without the federal government --- we have become less than sheep --- to be sheared --- and dipped --- and ultimately slaughtered and sacrificed on an altar of ignorance and sloth --- an altar of our own making.

"So, how do I propose to fix this --- I propose that we dismantle the Department of Education down to its last brick --- and return the money to our states, to our communities, to our schools --- and to our citizens. I want us to pay teachers what they deserve and control what our students learn in individual school districts.

"If you want your children to be stupid, then it should be your choice --- not the government's. But if we want our children to be their best selves --- to be brilliant at what they love --- then we need to have that choice at home --- and not to give it to politicians and bureaucrats.

"There is a cost to the education of each pupil --- that cost should be in the hands of a child's parents. Let the parents pick the best place to spend that money for their child's education. If our public schools aren't equal to the task, then let's have charter schools.

"Our children's lives are what we can give them --- they should not be the result of what the federal government and the D.C. elite want them to have. This is one of the most important steps we can ever take to reclaim our rights as Americans."

Porter looked across the stunned audience.

"Let's get back to --- a student, a teacher and a log --- and take the destiny of our children back from those who really don't give a damn about it."

CHAPTER 48

Dismantling the Department of Education was a shock to the political establishment and to both parties revving up for their political conventions. The White House Press Briefing the day after the President's address to the National Press Club was dominated by questions on the topic.

"What about Pell Grants for college students?" the A.P. reporter asked. These grants were the prime source of financial support for disadvantaged U.S. college students.

"They will still exist --- as will several other education programs --- but over five thousand bureaucrats and a budget over $70 billion dollars a year are not needed to deliver the few valuable services the Education Department currently provides. Remember, we've been seeing ads in magazines, on the Internet, and on TV to solve the problems of E.D."

The Press Room exploded into laughter.

"We just think getting rid of it is a better idea than treating it with drugs --- one of which is more and more money."

In essence that exchange reflected the tenner of the rest of the questions and answers. The President, particularly in light of the scandal at the Education Department, was adamant that elimination was the right answer to the corruption, stupidity, and political weapon the E.D. had become.

The next major news story of the day was the revelations of the connections between captured terrorists who had survived both the school bus and lone wolf attacks and refugee Muslim immigrant communities around the country. These isolated enclaves of refugees, mostly in Texas, California, New York, Michigan, Florida, and Minnesota, were made up of people supposedly freeing oppressive regimes. The one thing all these groups had in common was that they came from Muslim nations with the avowed goal of destroying the Great Satan, the U.S.

The program began in 1980 to deal with the influx of refugees from Vietnam, many of whom had supported the U.S. in the Southeast Asia conflict. The Vietnamese "boat people" were the beneficiaries of the original effort. Today it had evolved into the U.S.R.A.P., United States Refugee Admissions Program. Currently those who got the golden key to the U.S. were selected by the United Nations High Commissioner for Refugees --- largely filled by a group called the Organization of Islamic Cooperation --- a Muslim supremacist association.

The refugees were handpicked and without any input from the U.S. states, counties, or cities, were resettled in areas unprepared to deal with the resettlement of these people who shun American values. The sections of the U.S. were these people were located were usually places with little or no employment opportunities or public housing. The local school districts and medical communities were not equipped to deal with these non-English speakers much less the social, mental and medical issues that come with people from this other part of the world.

The young men and women were easy prey to Islamic Extremists who recruit them over the Internet in their native languages. This population, primarily supported by U.S. welfare and taxes, were turned into foreign fighters on American soil. That the trail from participants in the two most recent Islamic Terrorists' attacks led back to these isolated communities was an eye opener even to those who, through their church, had offered helping hands to enable the refugees to become terrorists.

It opened again the debate about immigration and how little control the U.S. was exerting over even legal new comers. Additionally the largely ignored or dismissed danger of Muslim communities which became very insular and militant, became a campaign issue.

President Randall felt this problem needed immediate attention. He addressed the topic in a Rose Garden ceremony to award Border Patrol Agents for acts of bravery on the job. After pinning on the awards, the President had these remarks.

"To enter any nation, especially ours, is not a right but a privilege. These men and women," Porter said gesturing to the awarded Border Patrol agents sitting nearby, "stand on the wall and protect us against the invasion of those who are not qualified. Every nation controls its immigration --- the U.S. is no different in this regard.

"We also understand that to be an American is an opportunity --- one you are either born with or you acquire because you earn it --- not because you committed a crime and got away with it. We have the right and the obligation to control our borders and those who both enter and leave our country. Illegally entering our country is not a human nor a social right. It is a criminal act."

His small audience applauded these words. These were words they already lived and served under.

"We understand that we are a nation of immigrants --- and we take great pride in that fact. But immigrants have the obligation to become a part of their new home --- to observe the established laws and traditions of their new home to the exclusion of their own.

"I find it extraordinary that I needed to issue an executive order to require legal immigrants to take the vow of allegiance to our country upon entering because many immigration judges and officials have, of their own volition, decided that a pledge to support and defend our Constitution --- or swear an oath to God that they will bear arms or perform noncombatant service on behalf of the United States --- was no longer politically correct..

"This should be the very nature and the task of immigration. If you fled your native country looking for a better life --- and you join us like so many have --- you must know that joining us means being a part of us --- not being *apart from* us. Our forefathers understood this. If you are unwilling or unable to make this promise --- you do not belong here."

Once more applause came from the audience.

"I want to be as clear and understood on this issue as I can be. Immigrants who refuse to become a part of the U.S. but attempt to alter the existing civilization here to match those of their former homes are not, in fact, immigrants, but agents of another power and will be treated as such."

More applause.

"Like it or not, this country was formed by white Europeans seeking religious freedom to practice their Christian and Jewish faiths. Our laws and our very Constitution are built on those values. While many today choose to feel our country offers them a 'freedom *from* religion', they are wrong. Our founding was based on a 'freedom *of* religion.' Our laws were written to allow people of any religion to come here and worship God as they see God. Those, who wish to change that in order to change our basic beliefs or to twist our laws to God and religion only to the way they see it, have missed the point."

This brought the people to their feet.

"Politicians who run and hide or choose their words to accommodate those who wish our nation and our laws were different do no one any service. They certainly do not serve those who have elected them. And yes, I know I say this, knowing I was not elected to the post I currently hold. That is the reason I can say what needs to be said and what needs to be understood.

"Cowardly acts of terrorism which grow out of our immigrant population are, in large part, the responsibility of that population. They always have been. The Irish coal mining terrorists, The Molly Maguire's of the 19th century, were the product of my own ancestors --- the Irish. If immigrants do not control their own, they bring down unwanted hardships and discipline on all their brothers and sisters. From the Mafia, to the KKK, to the Black Panthers, to the Jewish

Defense League, to MS-13, the Crips and the Bloods --- terrorism is terrorism --- and they primarily prey on their own. And yet, neither could they exist without the approval and shelter they were given by their own ethnic group. They represent their people.

"Am I saying, 'America for Americans' --- yes I am. But anyone who legally wants to become an American --- who has the desire and courage to do so --- can be one. Former Louisiana Governor Bobby Jindal said it best --- "Immigration without assimilation is invasion."

"We are taking in refugees, and not P.O.W.s, --- like other nations around the world, we need to have a place for these people --- particularly, if they don't know if they want to be here --- or to be Americans.

"We are ashamed of the internment camps in which we held Americans of Japanese origin in World War II. Still, if people are sent here without any skills, without any driving desire to assimilate --- without housing, incomes, or knowing the language --- and they are depending on us to provide for them --- let's do it willingly --- but do so on our terms.

"We can certainly do better than the internment camps of the past, but we should not be creating breeding grounds for domestic terrorists. By another Executive Order I have today empowered FEMA to provide housing that we can quickly set up --- housing of the type we offer our own citizens in time of flood and disaster. Many coming to us do not even know how to use an indoor toilet. They are NOT ready to go into American society.

"We can provide the needed language, social and job training for these refugees. We can see they have access to American media so they will understand what life here is really like --- not just 'Bad Boys' and 'Jerry Springer.'

"However, until they are employable, have a job, are self-supporting, have a place to live and sponsors to aid them other than the taxpayers --- until they are off the welfare rolls --- we should not deceive ourselves or them. They have come to the land of milk and honey but not without responsibilities. If they do not want to get off the dole, if within a certain number of months they are not ready to assimilate --- they are, by their own actions, deciding they would rather live in the third world and not in the U.S.

"Without work and an aspiration to become Americans they condemn themselves to remain refugees --- outside of our society. They are a burden, we as a Judeo/Christian nation take on with compassion --- but not unconditionally."

CHAPTER 49

"Randallvilles" were the name the media came up with to slam the idea of American refugee camps. They were trying to link them to "Hoovervilles" of the depression and to the internment camps for the Japanese Americans during World War II. What the media didn't expect was the resounding positive support that came from the American public for the President's Executive Orders.

The liberal media outlets and Internet bloggers were inundated with e-mail, instant messages, videos, as well as man-on-the-street interviews across the country from John Q. Public voicing support for not only the refugee camp idea but for the reluctant President, too.

Try as they would, the voices who wanted to censure the President could not gain the traction they had come to expect for their politically correct stances. Public opinion polls showed the country was behind the President by just over eighty percent.

Yet, before the story could play out much further than a few days, the headlines were grabbed by events at the Los Angeles National Democratic Convention. On the very first day, the F.B.I. swooped in and arrested a disguised Delilah Rome, and former Presidential advisor Bryce Brooks in different hotels near the L.A. Convention Center. Also publicly arrested in the lobby of the Convention Center itself was Yale Gallagher, the reclusive billionaire wearing a false nose, dark glasses, a hair piece and riding in an electric power chair. Of the Watergate group, only former advisor Willis Reiner eluded the net by staying in his secluded home in the Southeast Asian, non-U.S.-extradition country of Cambodia.

In Washington, the Attorney General, cowardly Winchell Hardwick, was also arrested at his Maryland home in the early morning hours.

The spokeswoman for the F.B.I. gave a statement saying that all the so called "Watergate Group," funded and supported by Mr. Yale Gallagher, had all been taken into custody --- including a former advisor to President Gibson and the current attorney general. The entire group was charged with "sedition, conspiracy, the attempted murder of President Randall in Milwaukee last year, and with treason." She also named the primary witnesses for the charges --- Presidential Physician, Dr. Leonard Millhuff and Secretary of State Victor Chesterfield.

Black, thin lipped, and mustached Gordon Lewellyn, the chair of the National Democratic Convention, came out with a statement that fell totally flat indicating that these arrests were "politically timed." It was obvious that the elusive billionaire, Gallagher and the others nabbed close to the L.A. Convention Center, were taken when the opportunity presented itself. There wasn't much else to say because the primary accusers, the Secretary of Defense Chesterfield and the doctor who had saved the President's life after he was shot, were known Democrats.

Democratic front runner, Senator George Tossen, could only say he trusted the F.B.I. and with charges as serious as these, it was perhaps unfortunate timing, but these suspects needed to be nabbed when they could be.

A shadow was cast over the rest of the Democrat's festivities as more and more information about the "Watergate Group" leaked out even past the final day of the convention. Tossen was selected as the standard bearer and his choice for a running mate was the Hispanic governor of Arizona.

The war continued, closing of the Department of Education moved into high gear, the refugee camps were built, staffed, and began to operate. News stories from the camps turned out to be ones of compassion and sacrifice by American aid workers and civilian volunteers. Clothing and other normal items of daily life were contributed and distributed to refugees and the children were seen smiling, going to school and playing.

Porter and Deidra were also discovering they did indeed need each other more than either realized. Life together, even in the pressure cooker and fish bowl existence of living in the White House was made easier when they shared an occasional M.R.E. lunch or their time together at the end of each long and demanding day. Deidra was quickly a fashion setter being a woman who was not afraid to get her hands dirty as well as being an elegant lady. Irene often appeared with Deidra at V.A. functions and the attention they brought to vets was powerful.

The President's staff could see a change in the Chief Executive as he sustained the diamond hard and razor edged criticism of each day but continued to be the leader the nation needed.

The week of the Republican National Convention in Nashville, Porter and Deidra went back to Amarillo to attempt to stay out of the spotlight. The President allowed Democrats in the White House who wanted to attend the D.N.C. in California time off. He did the same for those active in Republican politics. The shorten staff in D.C. was narrowed even more when the President and First Lady went to Texas.

Porter and Deidra had begun to talk about their time after Washington. Porter had been approached about a Presidential Library to be built at Texas Tech. Porter at first laughed at the idea.

"One or two books will make for a very small library," he said.

It was his newest advisor, Felix Alvarez, the well-connected D.C. attorney and deal maker who convinced Porter that regardless of how short his tenure had been, there was still significant historical importance to the documents and video of those days. And, Felix said, "You have done some things no President before you ever has. There are people with money who want to celebrate that. Don't think of it as being about you but about all the people who worked for you --- from Victor Chesterfield to Justice Karie Ann Cantu, to Dr, Regis Yablonski and Bethany Jane Battles. And don't forget your sister and brother-in-law."

"Okay. Okay," Porter finally gave in.

"Good," Felix said, "because there's already been $15 million raised. It'd be a shame to see it go to waste."

Porter could only laugh.

The week in Amarillo, particularly the evenings and nights were all about Deidra and Porter. They didn't even turn on the TV to see how the Republican Convention was going.

Thursday evening as they looked out across Palo Duro Canyon from horseback, balding Secret Service agent Bryant Polaski rode up on another mount from several hundred feet back where he sat on guard.

"Mr. President," he said lowering his arm from where he had been talking to the agents back at the ranch over his sleeve-mounted microphone. "You are needed back in the communications shack. I'm told it's important but not urgent."

Porter and Deidra exchanged looks.

"When is 'important' not 'urgent'?" she asked.

"It could be Page. Her water's broken or she's already gone into labor."

Porter reset his hat and they turned back to the ranch at a steady lope.

Inside the converted ranch shed, Press Secretary, Grant Yarbrough, stood at an angle to a wall mounted big screen video monitor awaiting the arrival of the President. Grant had gone to L.A. for the Democratic Convention and so was now with the First Couple while others made the Nashville political trip. As Porter stepped over, he saw his Chief-of-Staff, Graham Newcome and his Communication's Director, Cinnamon Hidgon standing together in a hotel room --- they were speaking through an Internet connection on a video tablet.

"Mr. President," Graham began, "they have just finished ballot number ninty-three here."

"And still," Cinnamon said, "we need to talk to you about it."

"I thought Vincent Sturges would have it sewed up by now," Porter said.

"So did he," Graham nodded.

"Sir," Cinnamon said, "Clement Nance would like to speak to you."

"I am not going to choose on this," Porter said. "What does Clement not understand about that?"

The freckled complexioned Chairman of the Republican National Committee stepped into view beside Cinnamon and Graham. In his raspy voice Clement Nance said, "The convention has voted to draft you, Mr. President. Will you be our nominee?"

THE END

THANK YOU

Thank you for taking the time to read *The Reluctant Incumbent*. If you enjoyed it, please leave a two to three sentence review here. It's important because reviews impact the algorithms at Amazon, Google and Apple. And they make a big difference to how a book gets ranked.

Word of mouth is an author's best friend and much appreciated.

Thank you,

Jack R. Stanley

FREE E-BOOKS

GET TWO FREE E-NOVELS
BY
JACK R. STANLEY

MURDER IN MULESHOE, murder in a modern small Texas town, and GUNS ALONG THE RIO, historic western action/adventure.

http://eepurl.com/dKEi_Y

ABOUT THE AUTHOR

Jack R. Stanley is an award winning novelist, playwright, and screenwriter. As an officer and combat photographer in Vietnam he earned the Bronze Star. Yet he says, "When you're in a firefight and everybody else on both side have guns while you have a camera --- you get to change your pants a lot."

After his military service he received both his M.A. and his Ph.D. at the University of Michigan in Ann Arbor in Radio-TV-Film. His doctoral dissertation was on the long running TV series GUNSMOKE. Stanley also received two of Michigan's most prestigious creative writing awards, The Hopwood Award, one for a one-act play and the second for a novel.

Still married to his gifted high school sweetheart, Stanley's first academic position was TV Area Head at The University of Texas at Austin's Department of Radio-TV-Film. He later moved to deep-south Texas and the Lower Rio Grande Valley for a challenging position with The University of Texas-Pan American. Here he taught Theatre-TV-Film for 30 years in the Department of Communication serving as Department Chair at U.T.P.A. for 11 years. He did take one year out to work for The University of Alaska Anchorage as a visiting professor. Back in Texas, Stanley directed for stage at The University Theatre, produced and directed fifteen student staffed, cast, and crewed feature films, writing most of the original screenplays. Just a few of his credits are available on IMDB.com.

He now lives in the Texas Panhandle where he writes his fiction and runs his blog, *www.TheFictionWritersNotebook.com*. His webpage is http://www.jackrstanley.com.

ALSO BY THE AUTHOR

Novels

The Reluctant President

The Reluctant Incumbent

Murder In Muleshoe

Corpse In Canyon

Through A Lens Darkly: Vietnam

The Lovecraft Murders

Guns Along The Rio

West of the Frio

The Gavel and the Gun

The Mormon Marshal

Short Stories

TALES FROM THE ALASKAN GOLD RUSH

Klondike Justice

Dangerous Camp At Kenai

The Winds of Skagway

Screenplays

6 and 10

Afternoon Delight

Angel's Revenge

A Violent End

Between Love And Murder

Blood Drive

Death Scene

The Defection of Grigori Dorsky

The Evil Eye

Fatty and Hearst

Gideon: The Horse That Saved Texas

Hell In Paradise

Hollowpoint

Holiday For An Assassin

Horse Thief Hollow

Incident At Lajatis

Love, Lust, and Life

Mom & Apple Pye

Pancho's Pilot

The Prometheus Peril

The Rape of Sarah Quinn

Seven Reasons Why

The Seventh Luger

The Texas Rattlesnake Murders

The Thing About Love

Too Good To Be True

The Vampire Rose

The Virgin Casanova

Plays

Antigone In Texas

Cyrano

The Last Virgin From Las Vegas

The Seven Keys

The Unwed Widow

Made in the USA
Lexington, KY
11 July 2019